Walter Kirn

THE UNBINDING

Walter Kirn is the author of five previous works of fiction: *My Hard Bargain: Stories*; *She Needed Me*; *Thumbsucker*; *Up in the Air*; and *Mission to America*. He lives in Livingston, Montana.

ALSO BY WALTER KIRN

My Hard Bargain: Stories
She Needed Me
Thumbsucker
Up in the Air
Mission to America

THE
UNBINDING

THE
UNBINDING

Walter Kirn

ANCHOR BOOKS
A Division of Random House, Inc.
New York

AN ANCHOR BOOKS ORIGINAL, JANUARY 2007

Copyright © 2006 by Walter Kirn

Library of Congress Cataloging-in-Publication Data

Kirn, Walter, 1962–
The unbinding / by Walter Kirn.
p. cm.
"An Anchor Books original."
"Originally published online at Slate.com."
ISBN-13: 978-0-307-27741-1
1. Technology—Social aspects—Fiction.   2. Information services—Fiction.
3. Electronic surveillance—Fiction.   4. Psychological fiction.   I. Title.

PS3561.I746U53   2007   ˈ
813'.54—dc22
2006026187

Book design by Christopher M. Zucker

www.anchorbooks.com

Printed in the United States of America
10   9   8   7   6   5   4   3   2   1

Introduction

In January 2006, Jacob Weisberg, the editor in chief of Slate.com, asked me out of the blue if I'd be interested in publishing a novel in his magazine. With no idea what I was getting into, nor any prepared material in my desk drawer, I told him to sign me up. The result is the story before you, *The Unbinding*—a serial novel written for the Web week by week and a section at a time and powered by a surge of naive faith in the capacity of cyberspace to do for long-form fiction what it has done already for journalism, music, gaming, and the graphic arts.

I started telling the tale in early spring with the intention of ending it by summer. The lessons came almost as quickly as the deadlines. Because the project had been announced on Slate as an "Internet novel," its readers seemed to have certain expectations. They were in the mood, I learned (largely from Googling the novel's title and scrolling through various blogs that cited it), for a display of technical bravado: links to other Web sites, pictures, video, and a whole range of multimedia tricks that I too believed would be helpful to the enterprise. An Internet novel, I thought when I began, should look and feel—and even sound, perhaps—like something new, disorienting, wild. A buzzing, humming electronic circus teeming with hypertext lions and virtual clowns.

But reality surprised me.

Within a few days of sitting down to work, I realized that the greatest opportunity offered to a novelist by the Web is not the ability to dazzle an audience with unorthodox content, but the chance to address it in real time, in something like the way that live performers do. The speed and directness of the electron could vastly shorten the long delays between composition and consumption that conventional physical publication requires. I could write a section on a Wednesday, send it to my editor (the impeccable and incomparable Meghan O'Rourke) on Thursday, and visit it on the Web on Friday morning. What's more, I could coordinate my tale (if I saw reason to) with current events. The week that a movie opened in the real world, it could also open in my made-up world. My characters could rush right out and see it, along with everybody else.

Of course, what's possible isn't always desirable. But sometimes it is. And this was one of those times, I felt, partly because the subject of my tale—the plight of what people used to call "the self" in an age of high-tech snooping, political paranoia, identity thievery, and Internet exhibitionism—had recently come to the forefront of the news, where it seemed destined to stay for quite a while.

Now, with some revisions, but not many, *The Unbinding* has been bound. It's a book on paper, between two covers.

Since a tale is not just its container, I believe, and can exist in several forms at once, I welcome this transition toward tangibility. Old-fashioned books remain more readable than computer screens (for now, at least), and they're certainly more portable. They also give the illusion of finality.

What books have more trouble providing is connectivity. On Slate, my text was just a click away from the nearly infinite library of the Web, to which it could almost instantly attach itself as it moved along. To re-create this effect in print (somewhat crudely, I confess, in the manner of primitive motion pictures or very early, very slow computers) a Web site has been developed for *The Unbinding* on walterkirn.com. The site lists the bold-type "link words" in the novel and allows readers to click them as they proceed. I recommend performing this little labor, although I recognize that it's disruptive. Fans of footnotes and appendices may not find it so, but people who relish the trancelike seamlessness of the traditional reading experience may retreat in frustration or disgust. That's fine. Ignore the links. The world these days (and not just the World Wide Web) is a realm of forking paths, of endless choices and alternatives, and we all travel through it by different routes, much like the characters in *The Unbinding*. And also, for that matter, like their author.

Always lost, yet always on our way.

Walter Kirn
August 2006

THE
UNBINDING

1.

They call at all hours with a thousand problems, and our satellites fix their locations to the square foot while our operators try to help them or put them in touch with specialists who can. They call because they've fallen and can't stand up, because they're alone and choking on their food, because they've been abandoned by their mates, because they smell gas, because their babies won't nurse, because they've forgotten how many pills they've swallowed, and sometimes because they're afraid that we're not here and crave reassurance in case they need us later. It's a costly service—sixty dollars a month for the Palladium Global Access package, not including the optional Active Angel Plan, which remotely coaches users through more than six hundred common Life Challenges, from administering infant CPR to negotiating the purchase of a home—and clients deserve to know we're at our stations even when the skies are fair and blue.

"AidSat?" they ask us, and as we answer them we check our screens for their pulse rates and other vital signs, which are forwarded to us from sensors in their bracelets or, for Active Angel clients, in their ear jacks. If the numbers look bad we press a lighted red key that sends an ambulance from the nearest hospital. If the stats appear normal we stroke another key that records and stores the information, shielding the firm from legal liability should it turn out that the sensors have malfunctioned and the caller is, in fact, dying on the line.

Last Thursday around lunchtime this call came. Peculiar, but not as peculiar as they come. The only reason to write it down is that I decided this month to write it all down, everything, my mornings and my nights, and to file it for perpetual safekeeping in the great electronic library of lives. I'm an interesting person, I've come to see. We all are. We don't deserve to disappear.

"I'm in my car. It's rainy—really foggy. I think I see a coastline on my right."

"How can I help you?" I asked.

"I'm lost, I guess."

"Humboldt County, ma'am, city of Eureka, heading south on **Wabash Avenue**. On your right you should see a Pentecostal church."

"Which state is this, though?"

"California."

"That makes sense."

"Do you need any further assistance?"

"No."

"You're sure? All conversations with AidSat are strictly private. You sound a bit frazzled, frankly."

"Time of month."

I let out a laugh I'd practiced and said, "No kidding," though what I meant by this I have no idea. Just trying to sound human, I suppose, which I'll admit can be hard for me sometimes. It's a skill like any other skill, and not the natural condition they make it out to be in the children's books.

The woman terminated our connection. But I tracked her vehicle for the next ten minutes. It's in the contract folks sign when they subscribe. If an operator has cause to be concerned, he's authorized to continue passive coverage without the client's spoken permission. I've made a habit of this practice. Three years ago, when I was new at AidSat, I took a call from the distraught head chef of a Kansas City country club who'd learned just moments earlier that he'd been fired. Since the man subscribed to Active Angel, I led him step-by-step through a scripted two-hour crisis-mitigation plan. I stood by in his ear as he ate a light, warm meal, obtained a pen and paper at a drugstore, and sought out a peaceful spot of natural beauty (a nearby city park I guided him to), where, in response to my whispered promptings, he sketched a series of detailed pictures depicting his hopes and desires for his future. He seemed composed after finishing the drawings, and, at his request, I let him go. I should have shadowed him. The man returned to his workplace with a handgun, randomly let off five shots in the main dining room (wounding no one but traumatizing many), then discharged the weapon into his own right ear.

Though AidSat provided me with intensive therapy beginning the next morning and lasting six months, the guilt still scratches, the regrets still bite, and sometimes my dreams light up with violet bursts from the bullets I might have prevented from being fired and never got to hear.

I followed the woman's vehicle on my screen as it entered the town of Eureka and then stopped moving. That was when her breathing suddenly accelerated and her body temperature shot up. She wasn't running, though. Slow, even steps, direction north-northwest, along a side street whose major landmark was a Salvation Army thrift store tagged on my screen as a high-crime locale. At AidSat we're not merely counselors; we're cartographers. Our trademarked multiaxis maps of America's physical and social landscape are the envy of the industry. They can pinpoint the safest neighborhoods for children, the highest concentrations of single black millionaires, and the most likely spots to contract a tick-borne illness. Location is destiny, is how we see it.

I fingered a key to buzz the woman's bracelet and waited twenty seconds for a response.

"What is it?" she said. Then a second voice, male: "Who's that?"

"We're checking back. As a courtesy," I said.

I heard the male voice say, "Fucking turn it off."

"That's nice, but I'm fine," said the woman, Sarah Flick, a licensed practical nurse, age thirty-four, and a resident of Saint Croix Falls, Wisconsin. I had her call history in front of me and saw that she'd used the service just twice that quarter, both times for relatively trivial reasons: to verify the safety record of a child's playpen she was buying and to ascertain the legal penalty for driving while intoxicated in Iowa.

"I'm really completely okay now," Sarah insisted.

But the health sensors said otherwise. Blood pressure that would pop the plastic screw top off a soda bottle. Light perspiration. A faint but discernible coronary arrhythmia. I touched the key that opens my conversations to my superiors at our Portland unit and lets them review developing situations. Sarah needed a medic, most certainly. I sensed that she might also need a cop.

"I believe you're in danger. Answer yes or no," I said. "Do you feel safe around this man you're with?"

"No." A quick and tiny "no," but vibrant.

"Is he threatening you in any way?"

"A lot of them."

"Physically? With violence?"

"Not so far."

"Could the reason you didn't know which state you're in be that he brought you there against your will?"

"He wants me to hand him the ear jack now, he says. He didn't know what the thing was before."

"Cooperate. We're moments away," I said. "We're almost there."

Such moments are what I live for in my job. They're why I get to work early for every shift and volunteer to fill in during the holidays: those times when I and the AidSat system unite—when the broad continental reach of our concern fixes on a single soul in peril and we stretch our arms down from the stars. Our infinite automated tenderness ought to have been built into the universe, and for a few years, as a child, I thought it had been. When my parents split up, I found out that I was wrong. But at last the flaw has been addressed. The **machinery** for answering prayers is now in place, and **I am** seated at its mighty **center**.

Two hours after Sarah's call, I heard from Portland—from a supervisor named Peter P., whom I'd dealt with once or twice before. I happened to know from AidSat scuttlebutt that he had come to us from the upper echelons of the personal wellness industry. It's a tame-sounding field, but in my experience it turns out some very potent personalities, including a young woman in my complex whom I once had the pleasure of watching at the paintball range where I blow off steam on weekends. Her name is Sabrina, she's shapely from every angle, and I happen to know through casual research that she works at the Heart Glow Spa downtown. We're headed for a date, I hope, as soon as I can finagle a chance meeting and come up with the right restaurant.

"That call could have worked in an ad," said Peter P. "The guy was her ex. Extensive prison record. He knocked her out with dope and stole her car and drove for two days before she woke back up. Only problem is she was wanted, too. Aggravated assault on the girl she left the ex for."

"Still," I said.

"I agree with you completely."

"We foiled an abduction."

"Sure as shit. The second one this week, my files show. Now, head on home. Your day is over, Kent."

I asked Peter P. why.

"New mental-health directive. You engaged in a high-stress intervention there. Depresses the immune system, we've found, especially in the winter and early spring. We're trying to be proactive on this front. Hit the gym, maybe. Take a sauna. Rest."

I did a few years at military school, so I recognize an order. Before I signed off I asked Peter P. a favor that I'd been thinking of asking him for months: a call history on this Sabrina cutie, who I'd noticed wore an AidSat jack disguised as a clip-on sapphire earring. He went oddly quiet for a moment, the way people do when they're writing something down, then offered to "dig a bit" and left the line. My impression was that her name meant nothing to him but that he wasn't entirely thrilled to learn that it meant something to me.

But that's my impression whenever I ask my colleagues for helpful tidbits on clients I'd like to **bang**.

2.

[By courier]

DVD/VID/PPV—Ref 467396 AD—Subject ID: Sabrina Matilda Grant

Aguirre, the Wrath of God
King Kong (original)
Little Shop of Whores
Deuce Bigalow, European Gigolo
Yoga and the One True Breath
March of the Penguins
Neil Diamond Live!

Activity: Norm
Educ/Soc Cult Index: Mid-Mid

Agent Notes: First porno all winter; guess she's getting lonesome. Otherwise, colossal yawn as always, only anomaly the Diamond disk. (Maybe her granny was visiting that night.) Urge immediate termination of coverage. Or termination of program, even better, because it's a SORRY INCOMPREHENSIBLE WASTE AND AN EMBAR-RASSMENT TO OUR GREAT REPUBLIC! Just joking, guys. Just frustrated. Just checking if anybody even reads these. OH, MY GOD, IT'S GODZILLA'S ENORMOUS FOOT ABOUT TO CRUSH A DARLING BABY MUSKRAT! No, didn't think so. Feel stranded here. Abandoned. This brat and her pals are inconsequential, promise. No evildoers here. Will keep at her, I guess, and try to stir things up, but because it's my duty, not because I'm buying this. (*Aguirre, the Wrath of God,* though—that impressed me. Maybe you're onto something I can't see. Cue Werner Herzog, cut to Neil Diamond? Maybe there are layers to this dope.)

I get tired of protecting America sometimes. I get tired of sifting the chatter to find the plots.

3.

[ExpressLink.com]

Dearest Small One,

Big news from Sabrina: I have another stalker. His name is Kent Selkirk; he lives across the courtyard; he drives an older black Ford minipickup with bumper stickers proclaiming that he's a Democrat, a paintballer, and that he'd like other drivers to, QUESTION AUTHORITY, FREE TIBET,

SUPPORT YOUR LOCAL SATANIST. On Wednesday I got a weird anonymous note quoting a diary the guy's been writing about some tricky scheme of his to go through my file at AidSat, where he works (you know: "AidSat—Always at your Side"), and use the info inside it to seduce me.

The funny thing—and the thing that makes me think the letter writer must know both of us—is that I've been eyeing this Kent since he moved in here. He seems like my type: a fouled-up jock with brains who goes around wearing flip-flops and pocket T-shirts and a ridiculous pair of thick dark shades that wrap around his head like plastic bat wings and emphasize the squareness of his huge skull. He reminds me of one of my crushes at U Mass, that guy who supposedly date-raped all the swimmers but wriggled off because of his top tennis ranking, except that he's less obviously psychotic in terms of his walk and posture and general aura. If he passes a dog, he pets it just like I would, and I've seen him hold doors for old ladies in his unit and carry a pregnant Hispanic woman's grocery bags. He also happens to be about half-gorgeous, with one of those partly caved-in boxers' noses, sprinkled across the bridge with sandy freckles. The only other thing I know about him is that early one Sunday morning at Starbucks, I noticed him reading a *Newsweek* in the corner and telling a girl whom he seemed to have spent the night with: "Forget the White House. Forget the

Capitol. If somebody wants to kick us in the *balls*, he should attack the Library of Congress."

Which all adds up to a favor, little sister. Is there somebody clever in your tech department, some nerd you can maybe bat your lovely lashes at, who can use this guy's name to find out what he's been up to before he spotted yours truly and fell in love? It's pure high school, I realize, and totally unfair. But it might be good for shits and giggles. Maybe that isn't how computers work, though. I wouldn't know. I'm just a facialist.

Well, it's time to head out now and do my Girl Scout's duty. Or maybe I haven't told you: I'm playing nurse. Every couple of days for a few hours I sit with this sweet older black man I met last summer during one of the volunteer mass searches for that poor little Hindu girl who vanished here. The guy got sick about five months ago, some vicious **new mystery bug** they haven't named yet (it probably started when someone ate a monkey). And mostly he just lies in bed these days making lists for his doctors at the VA of all the people he might have caught the germ from or maybe given it to. They're interesting lists because he's been around. He used to be a special army officer **stationed in Hollywood**, of all strange places, where I guess he helped out with TV and movie battle scenes and slept with all the nasty **nympho starlets**. He has a tattoo of a **dog man** on his left forearm, but it's all shriveled up and it looks more like a weasel.

But hey, guess what? In the courtyard now: It's Kent. I'm peeking at him through my kitchen window. He's just back from Costco, it looks like, with lots of boxes, and he's wearing his flip-flops because of the weird warm spell here. I'm thinking I'll change into a tighter top now and maybe freshen up my eyes and lips. I'll vamp him a bit when I walk by, but nothing desperate or flagrant—just scatter my scent. I'm still seeing Lorin, that fruity laser surgeon who gave me the massive discount on my eyes, but I think I've worked off my debt there (lick and nibble!), and I'm ready for someone less artsy, with a few hangnails.

Wet kisses until the end of time, girl,

Sab

P.S.: Finally watched that old Neil Diamond concert film. You're right; it has three shots of Dad in the front row, with a mustache and sideburns and the whole sad getup. And who's that beside him—that redhead with the beehive and the mole on her throat that looks all rough and furry? Maybe that's when he was separated from Mom, or maybe Mr. Stiff was a bad dog once. We'll rent the thing for his sixtieth next summer, put it up on the big screen at the party, and see if it gives him a second heart attack.

Now, help me get the lowdown on Kent Selkirk!

4.

[MyStory.com]

Before AidSat I had no self, no soul. I was a billing address. A credit score. I had a TV, a phone, a car, an apartment, some furniture, and a set of leatherbound Tolkien novels, but nothing that was worth listing as an asset on the do-it-yourself last will and testament I bought online one night four years ago after watching a medical program about mad cow. I had a mother, a sister, and a nephew, but none of them lived within five hundred miles of me, and the people I thought of as my closest friends—a guy from high school, two other guys from college—lived even farther away. And while I had my share of girlfriends, they rarely lasted for more than a few months, which was how long it usually took them to acknowledge that the "real Kent" they kept pushing me to show them (and accusing me of hiding from them) wasn't there, as I'd told them from the start.

Then AidSat hired me and gave me life.

And not just one life. Hundreds of them, thousands, attached to mine by fine, invisible cords that I can still feel on my skin when I leave work. It's one of the reasons I'd rather walk than drive these days—it doesn't shred the tender hooks and loops that fill up what most folks regard as empty space. There's no such thing, though, I've learned. The air is dense. The "nowhere" from which people think their troubles appear—the cars in their collisions, the tumors on their X-rays, the letter bombs in their corporate mailrooms—is, if they'd just pay attention, packed solid with soul.

What's happening with Sabrina is proof of this. I'm closing in on her.

It feels like fate.

It started when Peter P. sent me home last Thursday. My plan was to drop by the health club, grab a smoothie, and spend an hour on the ski machine before returning to my apartment and finally getting going on this journal, which I'd been putting off for the same reason I put off everything: a feeling that something else was more important. My problem was that I'd postpone those other tasks, too, and usually end up doing some needless third thing, which I'd leave unfinished when I realized it was needless.

At the health club, while I was changing into my shorts, I got to chatting with a new member, Rob, who, it turns out, is from Minnesota, too, and lives in the south unit of my complex. He told me he'd seen me in the parking lot and at the video store on Station Street, which is across from the building where he works. Rob's in telecom, a new outfit called **Vectonal**, and he sold me a low-cost voice-and-data package right there in the club while we were skiing. He also talked up an old movie he'd rented recently, a movie he said he suspected I'd enjoy because he couldn't help noticing at the video store how much time I spent in the foreign aisle.

I decided Rob had me confused with someone else (I don't do subtitles; I'll buy a Stephen King if I want to read), but then I remembered the way the foreign aisle snakes around into the action aisle and abuts the fantasy shelves. I asked Rob to describe the movie's plot, but he told me its plot was its "least involving element." We'd moved to the smoothie bar by then, and I sensed that Rob was talking for the benefit of the grad-school girls who run the blenders. He hadn't mentioned yet whether he was single, but he seemed as single as I was just then.

"I like the spot behind their knees," I whispered. "That's the skin that never ages."

"Because it's untouched by the sun," Rob said.

"By anything. Guys don't usually touch it, either. Women are virgins there."

"That matters to you?"

"At a certain level, maybe. I think it matters to most men, deep inside. It was obviously fairly important in the past, so how could it just have, you know, minimized? Evolution doesn't work that quickly." I studied Rob's eyes as he listened but I wasn't sure if they showed all the understanding I was hoping for. Then again, I'm not a skilled analyst of faces, perhaps because I can't see them in my work.

"Virgins still have all their *charge* in them," I said, laboring to refine my point. "They're like a new car battery. They *crank*. A guy turns their key, he can really draw some *volts*."

"Maybe we'll have to wait till we're in heaven. There aren't a lot of them left, that I can see. Maybe it's men's fault for letting them go to school."

We shared our first full laugh as buddies then, though it

wasn't a laugh I was proud of, or quite understood. Still, at the very beginning of a friendship, even fumbled attempts at humor should be honored.

"You in a relationship now?" Rob asked.

"I'm trying to be."

"That's sort of the air you give off. Good luck," he said. "Anyone special?"

"That's always the hope."

The movie Rob recommended was out that night, so I went back for it on Saturday morning on my way home from the Costco. The DVD was resting on a box full of lightbulbs and dryer sheets and Metamucil. While I was unloading my Ranger it must have fallen, though, because when I reached the door of my apartment, I heard a woman's voice behind me say, "If this is your disk, you have stupendous taste. I saw it last week with my film group. Stunning shit."

It was Sabrina, but dressed for the wrong season—in pink velour tracksuit pants and a green halter top. Her nipples were perked out like little thimbles, and her pants rode up tight and graphic in the crotch. A real anatomy lesson, and not a welcome one. Women these days have no padding on their frames, and when they thrust their hungry bones at me I like a little cloth to soften the onslaught. Still, Sabrina's mouth made up for everything. Her smile was like the flap on a white envelope: that clean, that even, and that wide. And glistening, like the flap had just been licked.

(Is anyone reading this? Write me if you are. It's **KentSelkirk@gmail.com**.)

We stood around in my doorway for a while and jabbered about the amazing movie coincidence. (I didn't let on that

Rob had recommended it, pretending I'd heard about it from a professor during my "student days in the Bay Area." It was a bit of pure inspired BS that I fear I'll have to back up now with more BS, like maybe a Photoshopped snapshot on my fridge showing me standing under the Golden Gate Bridge.) When Sabrina used the term "seventies German cinema," it put me on my guard. I'd slept with a girl in New York who'd spoken that way, and I'd found her unpleasantly stern and strict in bed, with too many rules about what parts went where and in what particular order and for how long. Her name was **Amy**, and she wrote short stories about her disappointments with men like me, who were the only men she liked, unfortunately.

Things got even scarier for me when Sabrina revealed that she grew up in Arkansas, the daughter of an influential lawyer who'd served as "chief counsel to Mrs. Bill" and now "represented some **other high-end evildoer**." I don't know what sort of records such men have access to, but after they booted me out of Cass Academy and before I landed at AidSat, in my stupid years, I kicked around with a crew of Saint Paul meth heads who smuggled damaged used cars down from Ontario and sold them to migrant grape pickers in Fresno. I did a lot of things like that. If Sabrina's father got to checking, some murky old stuff might come out about "Kent Selkirk," and I'd be good and screwed—not only with her but at my job. AidSat's a high-morality operation, and their puzzling failure to thoroughly probe my résumé was the act of grace that saved my life. (I don't know why I just admitted that. There's something about this machine I'm typing on that makes me feel that I can tell it anything, especially after midnight, with the lights out.)

I invited Sabrina inside, but she begged off, saying she had an appointment with a sick friend whom she cleaned house for and read to every Saturday. From the way she called this friend "they," not he or she, I guessed it was a man. She must have sensed my discomfort, since she explained then. She overexplained. This man, this Colonel Geoff, was well into his sixties, Sabrina said; he could barely get up off his mattress, and his illness had Swiss-cheesed his brain. Colonel Geoff was delusional, racked with fears and theories. The main one involved some event called "the Unbinding," which he'd hinted to Sabrina might take place soon but had refused to discuss with her in detail because people her age, he felt, had "faulty mind seals."

"Work on him till he coughs up," I said. "Sounds chilling. Or tell me more over dinner sometime next week."

"Only if you watch *Aguirre* first."

"I'll put it straight in when you leave. I'll watch it twice. Your silver earring there, with the blue stone?"

"My AidSat Angel what's-it?"

"I work for them. You ever get the willies in a dark parking lot, just ask for Operator Seven-S. I'll call in the SWAT team. Or I'll swoop down myself."

Sabrina didn't laugh or even grin, which is rare when I reveal my occupation and follow with that line. Instead she said, "Don't be grandiose."

"Why not? Why not, when I can back it up?"

We confirmed our dinner plans (when I asked her what

sort of food she liked, she answered, "I want you to use your ESP there"), and while she was swishing away across the courtyard, I spotted her peeking back over her shoulder as though trying to catch me staring at her butt. And I was, but not in the way she probably hoped. I was thinking that if she ever became my girlfriend, I'd lay down the law about modesty in dress. I've done it before with other women I've dated, and though they've grouched at first and acted ticked, I think they respected my judgment underneath. They knew as well as I, the AidSat operator who's been privy to rapes in progress and heard the screaming (and the silence when the screaming stops), that it's a rugged world out there. The more of yourself you show off to the wrong people, the more they'll eventually demand to **see**.

5.

[By courier]

Mag/Print/Lib—Ref 467398AD—Subject ID: Sabrina Matilda Grant

> O
> *In Touch*
> *Us Weekly*
> *Star*
> *A Is for Asphyxiate*
> *Trace Evidence*
> *D Is for Dismember*

Activity: Subnorm
Educ/Soc Cult Index: Low

Agent's Notes: More soul-sucking trash and lurid smut from the subject whom I once heard refer to her old college as an "extremely prestigious mini-Ivy" but who currently makes her living extracting blackheads and applying so-called "Dead Sea salt glows." Not that you give a flip, if you're still up there, and lately you've shown no evidence you are. But what if I told you a man our girl's been flirting with is a former associate of Karl OverGaard of Chisago City, Minnesota, a twice-convicted user of hard narcotics and an unindicted dealer of stolen firearms? Would that rouse you out of your bureaucratic slumber? And what if I told you further that our subject has been paying regular visits to a Lt. Col. Geoffrey Lark, a retired Marine Corps media liaison who, according to his service records, suffered three "pronounced factitious breakdowns" in the eighteen months preceding his discharge?

Would that perhaps move you to pick up the damn phone and explain why the hell I'm dogging these sorry dunces? These drab no-account middle-income **paintball warriors**?

Probably not. You've decided to let me drift here, subsisting on energy drinks and toasted subs, with half a million dollars' worth of gear irradiating my apartment with cancer particles that I can actually feel behind my eyeballs every night when I lie down in bed.

I'm at my wit's end, boys. I'm serious. I know things. I know how we do what we do. I know our methods. Don't you understand the risk you're running? Didn't you test my personality annually? Didn't you interview my fifth-grade

21

teacher? Didn't she tell you I'm irritable when patronized and positively flammable when ignored? But either you're not there or you don't fear me, because this packet got to you on Monday and now it's Thursday and I'm still here. In hell. Swigging NyQuil-spiked Red Bull and watching *Aguirre, the Wrath of God*, alone. For the fourth time this week. With the blinds drawn and the heat up.

A faint metronomic chirping in my temples, a contrapuntal twitching under my ribs.

I'm falling.

I need to get out more.

"Rob" needs friends.

6.

[Via satellite]

"Active Angel?"

"Present."

"Sabrina Grant. My PIN is 765432."

"Consecutive numbers. Not a prudent password."

"If someone's that desperate to steal some free advice, then be my guest. And take my problems, too. My cable bills, my cramps, my Nordstrom card, my eye-surgeon ex who won't stop leaving messages, the lease on my shitty new Hyundai—"

"Take a breath, dear. Excellent. Another one. Your systolic's just fine, but your diastolic scares us."

"I think something's happening to me. I'm not sure, though. It might be happening to everyone."

" 'Always Willing, Always at Your Side.' "

"What? You went all choppy suddenly."

"You must be standing near a microwave."

"I'm at a friend's, Colonel Geoff's. He doesn't own one. Could a Crock-Pot do it?"

"Unlikely, but why not step back from it in any case."

"I'm glad I got a woman. I like your . . . pace. Do you work with a guy named Kent Selkirk, by any chance? Medium height? Sharp chin with lots of shaving cuts?"

"Is he based in North Platte?"

"Where's that?"

"Where I'm based."

"No. Hey, can you hang on for half a sec? *It's not done cooking, Colonel Geoff. You should have soaked the beans first. They're rock hard. Just work on your list and I'll help you when I'm through.* You there still?"

"I can't break off unless you ask me to. And not even then, if I feel that you're at risk."

"Is it safe for my friend to bleed himself each morning? Not a huge amount, just a spoonful, roughly."

"That's your question for me?"

"It's my first one. Things are kind of piling up these days."

"Just a moment, darling. Searching. Reading. In most cases, if performed in sterile conditions, the practice is physiologically benign, unless it becomes compulsive or disfiguring. Barring that, certain ancient medical authorities believed it to be an invigorating regimen."

"Colonel Geoff learned it out in Malibu, he said. The stars do it. All the freakjobs on TV. He told me it regulates insulin production and helps you lose weight. Thing is, he's thin already. The mucous membranes inside his mouth and throat, they're peeling, they're chapped. They rub off if he chews solids. They thought it was lupus at first, but now that's out and they're saying it's something that jumps from person to person, but not through the bodily fluids or whatever, but maybe—please tell me if this is even possible—through talking a lot."

"Infection via speech?"

" 'Prolonged repeated intensive conversation.' He's batshit, right?"

"I'm searching. Nothing here."

"Would you look something up? 'The Unbinding.' Type those words in. Just for the heck of it. Anything?"

"Not yet."

"Don't sweat it. It's just some phrase that he's grabbed onto. It's like when you're six and you learn to say 'unique' and suddenly your teacher is 'unique,' your cat's 'unique,' your bike's 'unique. . . .' "

"To whom are we referring, dear?"

"This sick old marine whose place I'm at today. I'd tell you his whole warped story but he'd kill me. I'm not supposed to be making calls from here. He's phobic. No phone, no TV, no Internet. I think it's the pills. Or the bleeding. Still no luck?"

" 'The Unbinding'? Not a thing."

"Shoot. I was hoping you'd say it's from the Bible. I've been thinking it sounds like something from the Bible."

"To young people who've never read it, most things they hear out of old folks sound that way. My grandson thinks 'Eat your spinach' is from the Bible."

"That's funny. That's cute. I have to hurry, though. Here's my real problem. This guy I have a date with (that Kent I mentioned; he works there at your company, and no, I don't plan to sleep with him immediately; just dinner and drinks, though I'm not so sure he drinks; he might be one of those grim, clean-living types), he told me this morning when he asked me out that he studied in San Francisco once, at 'Berkeley College.' Which didn't sound right to me. And it's not. I checked."

"It's the University of California, Berkeley."

"Exactly."

"Did you confront him on his fib?"

"I should have, but I'd lied, too. About a movie. That eye surgeon I've been trying like mad to ditch, he had me rent it for him a week ago, but I never saw it myself. I said I had, though. I told this guy Kent it's my all-time favorite, actually. It changed me. Inspired me. La-di-da. I'm ass-fucked."

"When is your date? Do you still have time to watch it?"

"The trouble is that the movies this surgeon likes, I never understand them. They're way beyond me. And Kent's going to want to talk about it, probably."

"Can the surgeon explain the film to you perhaps?"

"I dumped him for good on my way to Colonel Geoff's here because I'd told Kent I wasn't seeing anyone and hadn't since my divorce three years ago, which was actually closer to seven months ago but happened way down in Daytona, so I'm safe. Plus it was an annulment, technically, which means the marriage never legally took place. Which means I can't misrepresent the facts about it because there aren't any. Gone. Withdrawn. Erased."

"An annulment on what basis?"

"We never actually had intercourse. Long story. My ex had anxieties. Me too."

"So why would you tell your new suitor you're divorced?"

"To make myself sound more substantial? More mature? An annulment comes off as an 'oops,' a silly slip—no scar tissue, no hard lessons, no inner journey—but with a divorce there's core emotional trauma followed by gradual spiritual renewal."

"Let's pause and summarize. Let's halt the mudslide."

"That's all I need. A halt. That's why I called."

"On top of seeking some stranger's admiration for cherishing a movie you've never seen (and doubt your ability to comprehend), you crave his respect for surviving an ordeal you haven't undergone."

"But know I will."

"The odds of divorce are only one in two, dear."

"Not in my case. I have different odds. I've learned from reading medication labels that if there's a three percent or greater chance of some uncomfortable weird side effect— blurred vision, say, or difficulty swallowing—I'm basically guaranteed I'm going to get it. That's who I am, I've learned. The failure rate. The person they print the warning stickers for . . . *I'm coming. I'm dishing the soup up. Hold your horses.*"

"It's time for you to go. He's hungry."

"Lonely. He gets depressed from working on his lists. Those were his golden years. Colonel Sunset Strip. You've been terrific, though. This really helped. Honesty. Openness. Clarity. Why not? Otherwise, what's there to love? The fear?"

"You're right."

"The cover-up? The performance?"

"No. You're right."

"Saying I want to talk to you again, how do I make sure I get you? What's your schedule? I feel like unless we keep this going here I'll lose my nerve. I'll turn all fake again. All shaky and fake, like before I left Daytona. Active angel? I'm turning off the Crock-Pot. You there? I'll unplug it. Are we connected? Fuck!"

"My code is **Operator Fifteen-F**. I'm here from nine to six except on Wednesdays. An eight-day vacation in Budapest nine weeks from now."

"You scared me. My heart stopped."

"I saw that on my screen."

"I just had a pretty wild, icky thought. Say that I do break down and sleep with Kent, and say that this ear jack flips on while we're in bed. . . ."

"I'll tell you a secret. It happens."

"Like how often?"

"More and more. Like everything."

"One more excuse to postpone penetration."

"Your 'anxieties' have persisted then, I take it."

"I think I've babbled enough for now. Good God!"

"Fifteen-F in North Platte, Sabrina. I'm here for you."

7.

[MyStory.com]

Occasionally, maybe twice a year, revved up after a hard-fought paintball match, I'll wash my face but leave my body spattered, concealing the "wounds" with a clean white business shirt that I button up tight around my flushed-pink neck. It's a ritual I've evolved, a private ceremony. I put on the tie and gray suit I bought for work and rarely wore after my training period, preferring looser outfits in lighter fabrics, and I head to the bar of the W Hotel, where the bands and athletes hang out when they're in town. There I order a single neat manhattan, amber and cold, with a ghostly sunken cherry. It was my grandfather's cocktail. I first tasted one at his Elks club in Racine, the night he celebrated his sixtieth birthday. It was also the night his only son, my father, flushed away his visitation rights by taking me out of state without permission to visit my grandfather and snagging a DUI on the drive back. I didn't see either man much after that, but I was fourteen by then, a hard fourteen, and convinced that I was the only man I needed. Now, of course, I'm the only man I have, which is why I try to go easy on the liquor. Easy on all those things. In all their forms.

But I do like a nice manhattan now and then.

Yesterday, Sunday, knowing I ought to stay home and watch *Aguirre* before my date on Wednesday, I ran to the range for a quick skirmish and suffered two gaudy fluorescent yellow "kill shots" during my squad's disorganized attempt to free a female peace corps volunteer from an urban terror hideout. It was a new scenario for me, engrossing and over-stimulating. The blindfolded "hostage," a guy in a blond wig, shivered my skull with shrieks and pleas that bounced at slashing angles off the tin walls. The match was held indoors, in a vacant old leased warehouse we've spray-painted roof-to-floor with hellish slogans. DECAPITATE! REVOLUTION! DEATH TO TRAITORS! Lots of brutal insignia and symbols, too. Sword-pierced eyeballs. Bloody talons. Entrails. The only rules are nothing Nazi or racist or anti–anything that really exists—no nation, church, group, idea, or individual.

With two exceptions. Two organizations.

Guess.

Click **here** for the first one. **Click** here for the second.

Maybe you dislike those outfits, too. Maybe you love them. Maybe you're involved with them. Or maybe you don't think about them any. But you'd abhor them if you only knew what sort of damage they're capable of causing. It's my secret, their crimes, and they have to stay my secret, because that's how the magic of curses operates. Call down destruction on something, then shut up. Desecrate its image, then veil its image. Wait for the crumbling. Then take credit for it.

Maybe those clicks will hurry things along.

Or maybe there were no clicks and it's just me here.

To gaze ungazed upon. I'll take the deal. It sounds depress-ing, but when you think about it, it's the same deal the cre ator gave himself. And the creator had all the deals to choose from. I believed that I did, too, back when, but somehow the thought prevented me from acting, which was why, for a time, all my choices went away. According to a **wise old priest** who counseled me toward the end of my decade of confusion (the man who steered me to AidSat, actually, and provided the reference that helped me land the job), the time to choose is always now, and the only two choices available are these: *Do* or *do not.*

"Do *what?*" I asked him.

"Anything." (He wasn't a conventional sort of priest.)

So after Sunday's paintball match, I acted. I dressed and drove to the W Hotel. I grinned the whole trip. I valet-parked. I winked at the floral arrangement in the lobby. Here's to you, white tulips.

Manhattan time.

Ten bucks for the drink and five bucks for the tip I hoped would coax the hipster bartender into pointing out a lounging celebrity. I'm lousy at spotting them on my own unless they're actively signing autographs. I don't admire them enough to memorize their faces. Most famous folks in the fancy magazines now could easily be switched with normal people who, after getting their hair and skin and muscles done by the California beauty experts, could earn the same millions, I bet. The same attention. Tom Cruise? Let's build ourselves a new Tom Cruise. Let's name the entity Jack Race. Then let's vote on our pick.

It would be a tie, I'm guessing.

But the bartender wasn't a gossip, or even friendly. I sipped my first drink in silence, frustrated, glowering at the five I'd given him that he hadn't bothered to touch yet. Sometimes they do that, as if it's not enough. As if it's just your opening bid. I contemplated removing it and replacing it with three linty, wrinkled ones. Maybe he'd notice and grab them. If not, I'd take away another dollar.

That's when my old girlfriend **Jesse** walked in. By the confidence she showed, I gathered that this was her regular watering hole. She had on a pair of tall X-laced leather boots that seemed designed for kicking in bedroom doors and giving seizures to fat old billionaires whom she was extorting money from. When I'd known her she'd been a hostess at Outback Steakhouse, outdoorsy and slightly windblown, a freckled chuckler, but now she looked combed and carved and oiled down.

"It's Cass," she said. An old nickname I'd used when dating, based on my initials (K and S). Back then, two years before I went to AidSat, I was demoing Vita-Mix blenders at fairs and supermarkets and trying to keep my day and night sides separate. A blender demonstrator is a performer whose corny voice and manner must be suppressed in casual social settings. The after-hours nickname helped me do this.

I bought Jesse a drink, as she clearly expected me to, and wasn't happy when it took the form of a twelve-dollar champagne cocktail made with a shot of dense bloodred liqueur that oozed and blobbed to the bottom of the slim glass and somehow held its beguiling swirly shape. Like the soul in the pit of the body. If there are souls. The priest assured me that there are, but that they're not inside us. He told me that's a misconception generated by the fact that it gets dark when people shut their eyes, and by our assumption that darkness always hides something. That darkness always has depths.

"What are you up to nowadays?" I asked her. My arousal made me feel sorry for Sabrina. I'd been cooling on her since the morning we made our date—ever since she'd looked back over her shoulder to see if I was watching her walk away. The glance showed doubt, which is one of my big turnoffs. The other one (which Sabrina also displayed, and at the very same moment) is the inability to live with doubt.

"I'm doing Marriott time-share presentations."

"Roping folks in with show tickets and things? I fell for one of those in Las Vegas once. A free steak-and-lobster buffet, unlimited trips. Except that they kept me prisoner all day first, filling out loan applications and studying floor plans."

"I show them a movie, and then they're free to leave. Anyway, I'm evolving out of it."

"Into what?"

"Forensic psychology. A master's degree through an online university."

That's when my plan to ask for Jesse's new phone number became a plan to focus on the rough, scaly patch that used to discourage me from kissing her neck. In young women, a sudden interest in criminology means that they've given up on finding love. Or more specifically, on giving love. I've run into two or three cases of this syndrome. The last was a late-night Active Angel caller who'd gone from stripper to arson investigator and kept me on the line for ninety minutes as she talked herself out of poisoning a pit bull that her new boyfriend insisted share their bed. Along the way I got her whole biography. It started with lots of church and whole-some team sports, took the usual downturn when she reached drinking age, and gravely worsened when she moved to

Florida, where—I've learned from our trademarked LifeSit maps, which measure things like level of sedative use and divorces within six months of marriage—the misery and mischief clusters once it escapes the small towns and medium-size cities. Those are zip codes I hope I never get mail in, seascapes I never want to see. Lean criminologists in string bikinis, starving pit bulls tied to stakes, Christians-only swingers parties. Florida is the rain forest of human behavior, with ten thousand times the rare species of other environments. Hawaii and San Diego are dicey, too.

I swiveled on my stool to check for ballplayers and saw, in a gloomy corner booth, alone with a Sunday paper and a dark beer, my pal Rob from the gym. Had he been there all along? I waved. He folded his paper, nodded, stood. There were bike clips on his trouser cuffs and a vee of what looked like freshly salon-tanned skin beneath the open collar of his polo shirt. I'd never estimated his age before, but I pegged it now as forty-six. A silvery, predatory forty-six that can finally afford what it longed for at eighteen but knows that it doesn't have forever to get it.

Jesse and Rob traded smiles as he walked over, and, before either one had said a word, I sensed a jagged mutual attraction, all lust and resentment and moral distaste, that I wanted nothing to do with. The genie in Rob called forth by Jesse's legs was not, I sensed, on good terms with the rest of him, perhaps because Rob had kept it bound so long. I expected that it would fight fiercely to have its way with him. And Jesse would take its side for her own purposes. Maybe to keep her closet full of boots.

In the ensuing small talk I made a point of mentioning

Sabrina, exaggerating my hopes for our first date in order to signal to Rob and Jesse that my interests lay elsewhere, outside the bar, and they should consider themselves alone together. I think they appreciated this gesture, particularly Rob, who encouraged me to draw it out.

"What's this girl's background?" he asked me. "What's she about?" That's when I realized something odd. Jesse, just moments before, had called me Cass, and Rob hadn't flinched. Nor had he called me Kent yet. Either he had a keen sense of discretion or he hadn't been listening when we met last Friday. He had an intriguing manner, Rob. Focused but not curious.

"Powerful lawyer's daughter. Educated. Lightly educated, but enough. Not bookish or driven, maybe, but aware. Cultural, too. Aspires to be, at least. Flirtatious but deeply gun-shy about relationships. On the edge of a breakdown that never quite arrives."

"And that's the part that interests you, no doubt." Jesse said this, but it came from Rob—her verbal translation of his arched left eyebrow.

"She claims she's divorced, but I checked and it's not true. She thinks that it makes her sound more worldly, maybe."

"So how did you woo this psycho?" Jesse said.

"By radiating bored contempt." It was one of those jokes that disguises a conviction. A conviction you'd find repulsive in someone else.

"So all you did was stand there? She came to you? 'Hello, there. Take me. But first let me tell you what damaged goods I am.' And that's appealing to the new .Cass, all spiffy and poised and cocktail-hour cool?"

"It's a special occasion," I said. "I died today. Two shots to the midsection. I shouldn't be here. I'm toasting my recovery from fatal wounds."

"Everyone here is toasting that," said Jesse. "That's what these swank hotel bars are all about."

She seemed to be speaking some version of Rob's thoughts still. They'd be in bed before midnight, not a doubt, and probably stay there until tomorrow lunchtime. Rob was a man who'd be missing a lot of work soon. Screwing and shoe shopping, dipping into savings, punching his tanning card three times a week. I could feel him already budgeting and scheduling. And waiting for me, whoever I was, to scram. He'd find me when he had questions about Jesse, after she revealed that we'd been close once, and this would create an alliance, I expected. It might even gain me a steady paintball partner. First, though, Rob wanted me to vanish.

He looked like a man who thought that he could will it.

But I still had to answer Jesse's question. "If two people aren't pursuing each other equally—at least in their thoughts, their dreams, in fairyland—they can't really find each other," I philosophized. "You guys have your next round on me." I flipped a twenty down. "On Sundays I try to get to bed by seven. Rest up for Death Day. That's what we call Monday."

Rob and Jesse squinted at me.

"When everything suddenly hits again," I said, "and people aren't in position, aren't quite ready. Asthma attacks. Bad accidents. Burst arteries."

"How gruesome. You'd best get on it, Cass," Rob said. Then he picked up my twenty, turned away, and called for a fresh bowl of snack mix and two more drinks. Without a glance back. Without a quick last question for the guy with more than one name and bright paint between his fingers.

8.

[By courier]

Web Search/Sum/Key/Hist—Ref 467398 AD—Subject ID: Sabrina Matilda Grant

1. "werner herzog movies" interpretations
2. **"dream analysis" worm**
3. "hyundai sonata" recalls brakes
4. "tom cruise" "deadly virus"
5. "yeast infections" homeopathy
6. "chronic yeast infections" homeopathy
7. "performance anxiety in women"
8. "dream analysis" kennels bookshelves algae
9. "rapid weight loss without exercise"

Educ/Soc Cult Index: Fluctuates

Agent's Notes: Sorry to send S's search list two days late, but pleased to announce that the next will be much tardier (if it's ever forwarded at all) due to abrupt, unauthorized vacation plans necessitated by urgent neuro-crisis, complete with ungovernable right eyelid flutter. I wish I had another job sometimes. I wish I hadn't signed on as a patriot. Because, frankly, I don't see a pattern in S's doings. I don't even see the potential for a pattern. This ding-dong lives her life the way that ants eat: from cake crumb to cake crumb to droplet of spilled juice to half-empty Coke bottle that it can't climb out of and sluggishly, rapturously drowns in.

S and her friends aren't bomb throwers, I'm telling you; they're the people bombers bomb. They're the decoys who make the world safer for the rest of us by sitting in crowded theaters sucking Starbursts and filling the seats at Kiss farewell-tour concerts. We need these sleepwalkers. To draw the fire.

In some ways, I'm awed by our achievement, though. We abide in evil times, undoubtedly, amid all manner of marauders, and yet you great sentinels have somehow managed to locate some last obscure inner sanctum of utter harmlessness. Sabrina's people. So dim they almost shimmer. So innocuous they terrify. What did you brilliant data miners do to come up with your suspect list this time? Cross-reference *Us* subscribers, futon users, humorous-greeting-card senders, snowboard owners, and eighth-place karaoke contestants? Then toss out all the high and low IQs and pick out holders of Old Navy charge cards?

I'll admit that perhaps this Selkirk, the girl's new crush, puts out a pale-lone-gunman vibe occasionally, but so do all these late-night gamer types who thrive on devil worship and Mountain Dew. So is that the next roundup? You're sure we have the resources? It's going to require interrogation cells the size of small Canadian provinces.

Anyway, off goes "Rob." I've met my dream gal. She's a potty-mouthed, smooth-skinned, size-two sociopath who shouts "Mr. President!" when I yank her hair and doesn't ask or answer personal questions. A grim little vixen, pure trauma in long dark stockings, with a yawning emotional crater at her center that not even Errol Flynn on crack could hope to fuck his way to the far side of. She's never been to Las Vegas but she belongs there, bug-eyed and topless, gorging on buttered crab, and I intend to devote at least four days to seeing if we can't devise a suicide pact involving French lingerie, massive doses of heroin, and front-row tickets to the Blue Man Group.

So no more commentary for a while—the automated feeds will have to do. As regards Miss S and Selkirk, they're dining tonight at a spot called Lucy's Sushi (as recommended by "Rob," their naughty Cupid), but I think they deserve some privacy, don't you? We were young and confused with infections of our own once. The world let us be, though. It granted us our moment. It turned away and let us cuddle. Kiss. Don't these two deserve the same consideration, no matter what threats the Bureau feels they pose?

Let's assume that they're bad, though. One or both of them. Or someone close to them, perhaps. And let's further assume that someday, someday soon, one of them dons a homemade Goofy suit and empties a vial of concentrated smallpox into the water cooler of some great theme park. We'll either storm in and stop this or we won't, but what will it matter if once, at Lucy's Sushi, in the glow of a hanging paper lantern, they spoke a few words of courtship to each other that we chose not to capture?

I'm thinking of going shorter.

It looks nice long.

The ends are a total disaster. They're dry and cracked.

More sake?

They say you should rotate your conditioner.

I use whatever's cheapest.

You're a guy.

American lives. Do we really want to know?

Me, I'm leaving for the airport now. I've packed up the blindfolds, the lubricants, the rope. Rob and Jesse deserve their moment, too. You probably already know we'll be at Caesars, suite 9890, with views and a Jacuzzi. But don't come knocking. I'll make a video. Jesse enjoys that. She's well-adjusted, really. If everything's bound to come out eventually, why draw the curtains? Just strip. Put on a show.

9.

[Via satellite]

"Sabrina, you might not have realized we could do this, so I hope it's not a shock, but this is your AidSat angel from North Platte dropping in to find out how you're doing (and how that big date of yours went, especially; you seemed so nervous about it the other day), and also to answer a question you asked me then. To be truthful, I'm growing concerned about you, dear. I've been buzzing your ear jack for several days now, and though I'm still getting your vital signs, thank heaven, I haven't received a single verbal response.

"I'm buzzing you again right now.

"I'm waiting.

"Well, that was fair warning. More than fair, I feel. You'll remember from your AidSat contract that if we have cause to believe that you're in 'jeopardy' (as defined on page seven, bottom paragraph), we're entitled to open your channel for passive coverage. Now, I could take this step immediately—and there's a faint voice in my head that's saying I should—but because we've formed such a personal relationship I'm going to give you another twenty-four hours to contact me and tell me you're okay. Two little words, 'I'm fine,' that's all I need. Though maybe you could explain your absence, also. Did our last conversation offend you in some way? Did you find me unhelpful? I hope it isn't that. I hope, to be honest, that you're on a spree.

"It's nothing shameful. I had my own sprees. I met my husband during one of them.

"Just don't make me activate passive coverage, dear.

" 'I'm living my life.' That's all you have to tell me. 'This young man I just met is sweeping me away.'

"But as to your question last weekend. 'The Unbinding.' I couldn't find it for you, you'll remember, but I put in a standing query and this popped up last Monday morning, when I started buzzing you. I have no idea if it's relevant. I'll speak the address very slowly so that you can write it down:

http://www.boston.com/news/globe/ideas/articles/2006/04/02/techno_thriller/

"I'll keep on searching, but I hope that's of use to you, Sabrina. At the least, I hope it proves that I've been thinking of you.

"This message will also appear on your computer."

10.

[USPS / four of eight pp.]

April 8

Dear Mom,

Over the years, and particularly in the last year, you've asked me many times to send my news in the form of actual letters—on physical paper, handwritten, not typed—so you can preserve them in your family scrapbook. Aside from a half dozen postcards, I haven't complied. I've never told you why, though. There are a truckload of reasons, but one main one: To have a family scrapbook, Mom, you have to have a family, and we don't.

I'm not referring to your divorce and how it resulted in you and I having ethnically incompatible, separate last names. Nor am I talking about my sister's marriage, which took away her last name and then failed, too. And I'm not revisiting your decision to sell the house I grew up in to a man who you knew would tear it down so that the other house he bought next door to it would have a larger, nicer yard with permanent deeded access to the lake. Followed immediately by your other decision to give up on three generations of Czech ancestors who saw Minnesota as the promised land and move to Phoenix and then to Winston-Salem, where I'm assuming that you'll still be when this old-fashioned envelope arrives, all fit for pasting in your scrapbook.

If you even keep a scrapbook anymore. It was a craze there several seasons back, and you, who've always been vulnerable to crazes, probably came to it late and dropped it early the same way you did with juicing, pyramid power, carpooling, lesbian-ism, Al-Anon, golf, *The Sopranos*, Ritalin, and fish oil.

My observation that we're not a family has nothing to do with you, however. It has to do with logic and reality. A human being can have only one origin, can only spring up from one conver-gence of lines, and this human being—without your knowledge, sometime in the mid to recent past—discovered that the lines that led to him were other (and higher) than mere bloodlines. Your "son" belonged to a family, he found out, that can't be reconfigured by the courts, can't sell off its home to some rich yachtsman, and can't be desecrated in a scrapbook that's probably lying underneath the stack of "dream journals" that you made me and Karla keep that winter after you caught us "rubbing" on Halloween.

Which is why I'm not going to describe this family, identify its **founder**, or tell you anything other than that it loves me and I try to love it back but often falter. What my new family offers me that our old one didn't, besides acceptance, a sense of duty, and the protection of an older male, is independence from all the other, false families—churches, governments, frequent-shopper programs, condo associations, census categories—that try to claim a person as he ages.

Your boy is free, Mom, and a threat—because these days, all free men are threats.

So, let's move along. My job is going well. We're about to get new headsets. That weird error I made on my taxes, it's still unsettled. My paintball squad's been invited to a tournament. And that lost, abused dog—the scrawny Basenji that our captain found grubbing squid behind an Applebee's—the dog we named Twist and adopted as our mascot and silk-screened the paw print of onto our jerseys—well, they're telling us that she belongs to a top breeder, that her real name is Gretel, that she was best in show, and that we can't ever have her back. She's registered.

Which they'll regret. We'll come by night.

Oh, and I met an old guy who knows Tom Cruise (whom I'd already been thinking about this week, and not in a nice way but in a vicious way) and who claims that he can get me or anybody as many tickets as we want to the Los Angeles premiere of the new *Mission: Impossible*. The fellow can't attend because he's ill (there was a tent of gauze around his bed as well as a grim little mine-field of bloody cotton balls), but he'll pay for the travel of anyone who'll go as long as they'll promise to read aloud his "blessing" (a tiny speech that he's still writing) to Cruise's pregnant wife. The guy insists she'll allow this. Cruise will make her. The guy is a veteran who met Cruise on *Top Gun* and coached him to angle his hips the way true aces do and show—in his eyes but not only in his eyes; in the depth and rhythm of his breathing, and even in the "esstex" of his complexion—the American naval aviator's boundless contempt for gravity and death.

It might be a kick, though I doubt I'll get time off.

It all depends on the unfolding of a story that I can feel developing around me. I can't tell you yet how it will come out, but I do know that it will come out somehow, and that represents an important change for me. My life has had many beginnings and endings, Mom, and almost every day I seem to go directly from false start to anticlimax, but so far I've never experienced this feeling of being in the middle of something. Centered.

[three pp. to follow]

11.

[USPS—cont'd]

It started four days ago, last Monday night. I was taking a facialist to eat sashimi. I'd had a crush on the woman since January, and we'd been swapping vibrations at our complex. Things heated up between us when, one weekend, at a new acquaintance's suggestion, I rented a German epic about conquistadors that happened to be the facialist's favorite film. She spotted me carrying the disk to my apartment, we talked a bit, we realized we had a lot in common, potentially (especially if I watched and liked the movie), and so I asked her out for Japanese food after learning from her AidSat file that she'd been hospitalized on New Year's Eve for a violent digestive episode that she blamed on consuming spoiled raw fish.

On our drive to the restaurant we stopped at the apartment of the phobic old colonel who tutored Tom Cruise, where the facialist feared she'd left a Crock-Pot on. She'd met the colonel while helping with the search for that allegedly kidnapped teenage girl whose story went national for a time last fall, with the relatives spreading out across the morning shows (lovely, soft-spoken, trusting immigrants who flinched under the lights) until the TV people got annoyed with them over their refusal to show photos of their missing daughter's face. (Photos were against the family's religion.) When a newspaper later reported that the girl had been pledged in some ritual to an older man who taught at a college here once but lost his job for claiming that our government still kills Indians and that it dropped an atom bomb on Egypt but hushed it up with a transfer of gold bouillon, the public decided that the family wasn't worth helping. The girl has never been located, but the facialist and the colonel still think about her.

As we were leaving his apartment, I felt my cell phone shudder in my pocket. It rattled again while the facialist and I were chopsticking up small slabs of slippery tuna and discussing movies and the universe, the way people do on uncomfortable first dates. About the movies we agreed that *Aguirre, the Wrath of God* may be the greatest tragedy ever filmed, though neither of us could explain exactly why. About the universe we had this exchange:

"I feel sometimes," the facialist said, "like I've woken up in a dark room and I'm walking with my arms stretched out, trying to find the walls."

"Succinct," I said.

"But what do I do when I reach the walls?" she asked me.

"Try to climb over them?"

"What if they're too tall? What if the walls go clear up to the ceiling?"

"Then sit on the floor and wait for them to crumble. All walls do, eventually."

"But what if I die first?"

"Your ghost can just pass through them."

"But what if there aren't ghosts?"

"There have to be," I told her. "Why would there be

walls," I reasoned, "unless there were also things that could pass through them?"

"Eat that last nice hunk there. It's for you."

"Do you believe in walls, Sabrina?"

"Walls are all I believe in, I'm afraid."

"Then," I explained, "you also believe in ghosts."

During this talk my cell phone jumped a fourth time, but I didn't pick up the messages until I was sitting on the facialist's mattress, waiting for her to wash up and brush her teeth. It was one in the morning. We'd jabbered for four hours. Once you really get to pondering, walls and ghosts are an enormous topic.

Message one: "This is Jesse. Call me back."

Message two: "You need to call. It's Jesse. I'm in Las Vegas. I'll be up all night."

Remember Jesse, Mom? The windburned sailboarder from Outback Steakhouse whom I bought an engagement ring for after three weeks? Who dumped me for the Don Juan who built log homes? She's an official W Hotel slut now who rubs that glittery makeup in her cleavage and can have any man she points her nukes at.

Message three: "You have to call immediately. I'm down here with Rob, from the bar. He's in the poker room. I was scrounging for Advil in his overnight bag and I found some things you need to know about. I care about you. I'm anxious for you. Call me."

Who this Rob is doesn't matter, Mom—just a guy from my complex (who recommended that movie). What matters is that Jesse mistreated me and that I take calls for a living, all day, all week, and I'm required to answer every one of them. But I didn't have to answer hers—not with a cute facialist right there (and a late-blooming technical virgin, I happened to know) who seemed, from all the electric brushing noises and toilet-flushing to-do and bathroom racket, as though she were preparing the sort of circus that veterans like Jesse don't have to show a guy, since all they need to do is smoothly clench.

Though it wasn't a circus I'd want to join each night (and maybe the facialist sensed this, and it hurt her, and that's why I haven't heard from her this week), at least it convinced me when I heard message four (after kissing the facialist good-bye and noticing that her copy of *Aguirre* was still immaculately bagged) that I didn't have to give in to temptress Jesse. No matter how deeply I realized that I still loved her.

Message four: "Rob has copies of your journal entries from MyStory.com. They're paper-clipped neatly together in a blue envelope. In one of them he highlighted the word 'Nazi' with pink fluorescent marker."

Well, at least one **sick fool**'s reading me, I thought. I'd better put in more stuff about the gym. About how I never launder my skunky shorts. About how I get noble stiffies in the hot tub from imagining my paintball team vanquishing the breeder who took our mascot.

Then, a day later, this call came. From Rob.

"We need to discuss your ridiculous ex-girlfriend. Not right away, but when I'm there again."

"I'm flattered," I said.

"By what?"

"By all of this. Whatever it is. This increase in activity."

What I'm saying here, Mom, is that I've gone for years keeping my head down, minding my own beeswax, and drawing no attention from the world. But I've begun to matter in recent days. My life has begun to mesh with other lives, maybe even to drive them. And I like it. Because, though I can't tell you how yet, I've been preparing for it.

Now stick all of this in your scrapbook.

Love,
Your kid

P.S. At work they're producing a series of radio ads featuring actual recorded calls, and one of them (as of now, at least) will be an artistically edited tape of me helping a panicky New Hampshire babysitter smother a grease fire in a toaster oven. And that's the last real letter I'll ever write you.

12.

[DrudgeReport.com]

MISSION IMPLAUSIBLE 6?: Classified info from stolen Pentagon laptop indicates that Cruise, Madonna, Osmond, Nicks, Diamond, Reagan, Olivier, and others are "spiritually bewildered zombie sex pawns" in decades-old joint U.S.–U.K. operation to infiltrate, manipulate Hollywood. Source: "It was trickier getting in their pants than getting inside their heads." Developing hard . . .

13.

[FedEx]

Hey, Dad,

I'm sending this by FedEx. I'm not sure why. I've always trusted FedEx. I'm not sure why. Maybe because they deliver frozen plasma. Or maybe because you never hear of FedEx drivers suddenly gunning down their supervisors. I dated one once and the guy had spirit, pride. I got the feeling he cherished his packages and would rather have crashed through nineteen guardrails than let his van be hijacked or tampered with. I envy the small, pale Mormon girl who married him. They live across town in a house with foil pinwheels spinning merrily in the petunia beds. Trikes in the driveway. Campaign signs in the yard. Growing up in a house full of globes and bound *New Yorker*s and important Kennedy collectibles, I thought I was above such happy crap, but as a single thirty-year-old facialist, I'm turning into a lawn ornament myself. Driving home from the spa some evenings, fried from exfoliating surgeons' girl-friends, I park across from the driver's kitchen window and watch his family saying grace. They eat by candlelight—always. And guess who hurtles up to do the dishes?

Inside this mailer you'll notice a sealed envelope. I can describe what's in it, but you can't open it. I need you to store it safely at your firm, wherever you keep the secret affidavits, murder weapons, sacks of Krugerrands, and all the other crap I know you stash there. The papers in the envelope belong to Lt. Col. Geoffrey Lark, whom you should consider a new client, with all the sacred privileges you grant to embezzlers from UNICEF. The papers contain a partial list of potential infectious contacts—including notes on how the contacts happened—that Colonel Lark has been dictating to me. The dollar bill in the mailer is your retainer.

Seeing as it was my birthday two days ago, you've probably been trying to reach me. I'm holing up here at the colonel's place, sad, incommunicado, and secretarial. We eat lentil soup behind drawn blinds. Sexually active young men creep by outside, tracking my scent, pinging pebbles at the windows. I break their toes like snap peas in my dreams. The colonel tells me that at the Playboy Mansion he once found himself alone with Stevie Nicks in a bare ceramic-tiled room fitted with mammoth pewter showerheads and, in the floor, a star-shaped golden drain. He asked Nicks what she wanted from him in there. "A thorough soiling and then a thorough rinsing."

I've been soiled, Dad, but I'm still unrinsed.

Don't stress about my physical safety, though. The AidSat ear jack you bought for me the summer I drove cross-country in the Acura to check out Yellowstone and Aunt Flipper's ranch is technically still operable, even though I ignore the voices pressing through it out of respect for Colonel Lark's belief that speaking to anybody you can't see is like pouring your "esstex" down that golden drain.

Esstex. A word he made up for a "fresh testament" that he says was written on a frigate anchored a mile off of Catalina Island and staffed with silent Fijian masseuses who dug at the lumps in the officers' hunched shoulders as they brainstormed up new gods. "We made brutal miscalculations," he admits, "but we had our breakthroughs, too." He wishes his masters would call him back to work. There were more funds for such projects once, he says, but now all the cash goes into avionics and "smart" artillery shells— now that good **"myth-ops"** might actually save nations.

My bitter sniffles are piddling next to his, Dad. His face when he thinks back and worries forward sweats and melts and streams like a hot Popsicle. I dab it with refrigerated Wet Ones. I kiss away the drips. He's finally letting me in, and it's an honor, even though I know he lies a lot. No one can be as important as he remembers being, or as feared as he feels he is now. He trusts me, though, like I trust FedEx. Like I can still trust you, I hope.

Your girl but no one's woman yet,

Sabrina

P.S. I saw a film of you grooving away at a Neil Diamond show next to a fox who wasn't exactly Mom. It's cool, I guess. It's cool except for how caught up you seemed in "America." It's not really Diamond's song. They forced it on him. In a Reno hotel at 4:15 a.m., on the balcony of a twenty-first-floor suite. The choice they gave him was jump or make a hit of this. Diamond asked for his glasses. He read the **lyrics** they'd written. Then the colonel handed him a guitar.

14.

[MyStory.com]

Daylight saving time saves no one. It's spring, when people uncoil and make mistakes. At AidSat, we pump up the lumbars in our desk chairs as our overstimulated callers plunge over muddy embankments in new sports cars, weep uncontrollably in motel bathrooms while drunken lovers pound the doors, and vomit into restaurant urinals after gorging on stuffed-crust pizzas that they pledged at New Year's not to eat again. It's been a siege at work these last few days—no lunch breaks, no chats over coffee, no, just the relentless application of empathy to hundreds of seasonal breakdowns that we saw coming the moment more sunlight was added to the evenings. One man from Columbus whom I counseled on Wednesday overdosed on allergy capsules and then spotted the Savior, dressed in a black trench coat, gathering daffodils in his backyard. I read to him from a script on my computer screen devised to calm outbursts of religious mania.

"Sit down with a cold glass of water and your scriptures, picture the face of your mother or your best friend, and say to yourself: 'At my next meal—' "

"Is this Gospel of Judas authentic?" the fellow asked me. "Where did they find the thing? And when, exactly? My girlfriend says it's been lying around for ages."

"I believe it's an old gnostic text."

"So that's official?"

My cell phone filled up with messages as I worked. Three or four were from Jesse, who'd left Las Vegas with Rob after he'd won tens of thousands in a poker tournament. He'd impulsively leased a Cadillac convertible and driven them through the night to a resort in Laguna Beach. They were eating raw foods, she said, and getting massages meant to sweep the toxins from their muscles. He'd confessed to her that he'd been reading my online journals (Hi, Rob! Come back to the gym for a long sauna!) as part of a "hush-hush effort" at Vectonal to perfect a new telecom product known as MeNet that would compete with AidSat in the market for "seamless life-assistance interfaces." I didn't call Jesse back, but it was hard to contain my curiosity after she informed me in another call that Rob had drowsed off one afternoon during an in-room couple's hot-stone massage and muttered the name "*Aguirre.*" Jesse knew of the film from the printouts of my diaries, so she confronted Rob when he woke up and was warned—with a vehemence that she said alarmed her—that any more questions relating to me, my writings, AidSat, MeNet, or Rob's Vectonal job would land her in "grievous bureaucratic peril," beginning with registered letters from the authorities about her chronic underreporting of tips during her career at Outback Steakhouse.

(Note to Rob: For someone I've only hung out with a couple of times, your fixation on me is pronounced, and your explanations for it laughable. I dealt with a few of you haunted AC/DCs during my two years at military school, and let me advise you that roaring around the West playing Texas Hold 'Em with fellow degenerates, champagning and Saks-ing my cash-strapped former lover, and ordering room-service rubdowns from hotel healers won't bring your restless soul the peace it seeks. Accept yourself, Rob, and find a good support group. Or call me at work—we maintain extensive directories.)

The next cluster of urgent voice mails came from my paintball squad's captain, Colin Frisch, instructing me to initiate phase three of our plan to liberate the imprisoned show dog Twist, whose case I've been reluctant to discuss here out of fear of jinxing our plot. But my shyness, I now realize, has served no one. And especially not you, Rob, my unbalanced but only identifiable reader. You deserve to know more fully the humane yet lively adult male whom, for whatever questionable reasons, you furtively adore.

Phase three in our plan to set free poor Twist—the run-away, Dumpster-diving **Basenji** that brought our squad such luck and joy last winter after we found her and nursed her back to plumpness and before she was torn from our embrace by Stan and Tammy Kurtz of Canine Endeavors, her greedy AKC-backed breeders—began last Thursday night, when I summoned two teammates through their AidSat ear jacks to meet me at Fuddruckers in the Northgate Mall. "Aaron" and "Storm" dined lightly, on chicken sandwiches, as we mapped on a napkin the parallel dirt roads that form the northern and southern borders of the rural CE kennel complex. We'd been scouting the operation for months, observing the feeding and exercise routines there, noting the bedtimes of its owners, and recording the comings and goings of various service personnel.

Our task that night was to engineer a meeting with a pair of male and female cleaners who were the last folks to leave the place most evenings. They appeared to be Mexican, middle-aged, and married. They drove a retired Ford Galaxy police car with a stretched and duct-taped garbage bag for a rear driver's-side window. The man dipped snuff. The woman dragged her left leg and seemed religious, compulsively crossing herself as she raked cedar chips across the filth and stench of the locked run where Twist paced listlessly behind the chain-link.

I sat with Storm in my Ranger and watched them clean as Aaron, who'd ditched his Jetta on a side road, belly-crawled up behind their Galaxy and pricked a slow leak in one of the rear tires. The plan was to follow them when they drove home, pull alongside them when the tire gave out, offer aid, and get to talking. We assumed that the pair was disgruntled and corruptible.

"I think I hear sad little Twist," said Storm. "She's lonesome."

I listened. Whichever dog was howling, its cries conveyed the pain of the whole pack. Above the kennels and the surrounding dairy farms, whose cooped-up miseries gave off no sounds but fouled the truck's air vents with sickly greenish odors, hung a waning, pollution-rouged half-moon. Twist would be free before the orb was full again—that was my vow, which I made out loud to Storm. He held up two fingers and crossed them. He knocked wood. Storm is a serious amateur astrologer who hosts a late-night call-in show, *Ethereon,* on the state university's public radio station. He cast Twist's natal chart using Kennel Club records and warned us that all the Neptune in her essence might hamper our mission.

Storm's pessimism irked me. From what I know of the occult, it's supposed to empower human beings, not provide them with more excuses.

The cleaners drove off in their Ford at 9:15. Their deflating back tire stirred up extra dust that clouded my headlight beams. They didn't stop, though. I pulled up closer and flashed them. They didn't slow down. The paved highway was only two miles ahead, but our goal was to corner them away from traffic. Then Aaron gunned past me in his Jetta, waving a hand as though to say *I'll handle this.* I braked to give him time. A minute later there we were, offering jacks and flashlights to the cleaners.

And there was Twist, up on his hind legs in their backseat,

startlingly, inexplicably accessible and nearer to freedom than we'd dared hope. Spooky Neptune had shed an unexpected influence.

"Your dog?" Storm asked the woman in Spanish. I couldn't translate her answer, but it was long and included the English words *vaccination booster*. The man and Aaron had raised the car a foot or two, but the jack was sinking and tilting in the damp ground. The morons kept on cranking. The car slipped sideways, shuddered, and settled, trapping the jack beneath a rusty brake drum. Twist's frightened scratching had ripped the garbage bag and put her in a position to leap and flee, her front paws perched on the glassless window frame. I tried to push past the woman to grab hold of Twist, but an error in footwork tripped me, I bumped Storm, he reached out and touched the car to keep from falling, Twist squirted out, the chassis shifted, groaned, and when it rocked down off the fulcrum of the jack, the tortured yelping drove ice picks through my chest.

The cleaning woman let loose a third-world scream that could have shaken the cross from a cathedral, and Storm, the doomsayer, fled—in Aaron's Jetta. Permanently disgraced and off the squad.

Aaron knelt in the dirt consoling Twist, whom he'd pulled out from underneath the car and who was sitting up now, very straight, all purebred and obedient, holding out his mangled right front leg as though inviting somebody to shake it.

Leaving me to call AidSat.

I identified myself using my employee code to the randomly selected operator, whose code I asked for in return. The woman's prefix indicated that she was stationed in

Nebraska, at the new North Platte Special Routing Facility, which specializes in mental-health emergencies among a selected group of high-risk clients who aren't aware of having been so identified. Because of the late hour, North Platte must have been experiencing a lull and taking on nonspecific system demands.

"We've got about three separate challenges here," I said. "No law enforcement, though. You got me?"

"Yes, dear." That's how all those special North Platte ops talk. Soothing. As though you've reached them in their rocking chairs. All older, all female, and all intensively trained. Former military nurses, most of them.

"We'll need a wrecker, a fluent Spanish speaker, a veterinarian, and three hundred dollars in cash."

"All on their way."

"Been busy this week?"

"Flooded."

"Especially Michigan residents, I've been noticing."

"I blame the new round of layoffs at the Big Three."

"They certainly don't help much."

And in no time, half an hour, it was done. Twist had been disinfected, bandaged, and splinted. The ruined tire had been replaced. The cleaners' immigrant silence had been bought. When I dropped off Aaron at his condo, we argued over possession of the dog, but I prevailed by pointing out my lack of a roommate and my higher salary. Twist rode in my lap back to my complex and slept on a throw pillow beside my futon with one of my arms stretched protectively across her. I didn't sleep. I listened to her breathe. She must have been dreaming, because she jerked a lot. Sometime during the night I woke up crying. I phoned Sabrina and left a message admitting that I'd been abrupt and cruel to her after our night of pricey sushi, lofty conversation, and awkward breachings of her aging hymen. I begged her for another chance. Caring for a crippled pet, I told her, had softened me inside.

"Come out, come out, wherever you are," I said.

And because there was a small dog involved, she did.

15.

[By courier]

Agent's Memo: In the grounds at the bottom of her low-fat lattes? In the stains underneath her polyester mattress pad? In the S-curves and loops of her discarded dental floss? Where was it written? And why couldn't I read it? And why can I discern it so plainly now, from so far away, in this dim and silent room where I'm sitting naked on the floor encased in a tightening rind of drying mud and breathing the fumes from a dish of burning oil whose wan blue flame is just moments from going out?

I see the plot now because I want to see it. Maybe that's what's changed.

The truth is simple: Sabrina Grant and Kent Selkirk, I know now (and might have known before, had I not been so desperate to find "proof") are the deeply embedded, plain-clothes vanguard of an immensely dangerous new foe whose goals are murky even to its members. What makes our job so much harder than it should be is that these moronic shadow soldiers don't view themselves as soldiers at all, but as harmless average citizens. Nor do they regard their orders as orders; they experience them as impulses and notions formed independently in their own minds. No wonder this adversary baffles us. It's like none we've ever faced. It can't be subverted because its loyalists aren't aware of being loyal to anything other than their own vague instincts. Its instructions can't be intercepted because they're never formally issued. Its commanders can't be captured because they don't, in fact, command.

Do I have it right? Is that a fair description? A volunteer strike force of the unaware executing a plot that they can't fathom? But which we're in the process of fathoming for them, so that we can foil it just in time? (By election time, ideally, when we foil most plots. Or announce to the world that we've foiled them, that is.)

I'm back on the team, boys. I'm rested and I'm ready. Outlook: open. Attitude: adjusted. Disbelief: suspended. Hammer: cocked.

They annoy me, these kids, and it's time to make examples of them. "Guilt" is an obsolete category, anyway. Guilty is as guilty acts. Let the **Trap-and-Trace** show trials begin!

But here's what I need to complete my mission: your patience. I'm not on station at the moment (I'm knotting the belt of a clean white terry bathrobe and padding in hemp slippers across a hallway to ask my new gal pal if she's finished with her pedicure), but I've started to realize that physical proximity isn't needed to follow this new movement. The scanning devices we use are highly portable, and the signals scattered by the enemy fill the atmosphere from pole to pole. Indeed, the farther away one moves from the signals' specific points of origin the more telltale they become.

And odd little victories occur at random. To wit: Out of some lingering sense of loyalty to a man she's described to me, three times, as "gravy without a biscuit," my flighty young slut decided the other day to warn Mr. Selkirk about my interest in him. This only caused him to boast and joke and showboat in an attempt to hold my gaze. He even confessed to a small theft (the abduction of a dog) that I'm considering reporting to his local police department. He also showed vulnerability to blackmail. In mocking what he took to be my predatory bisexuality, he displayed a knowledge of the tendency that can be gained only by having it.

I'm finally having fun, is what I'm saying. I'm getting my patriotic spirit back.

But here she is! Behold: mauve toenails. And no more calluses or cracks. Toting a pretty silk gift bag full of lotions that are complimentary but not free, as men understand but women never will.

"I'll call for the car," I say. "We'll swing by Nordstrom. Grab my amber Ray-Bans from the room and six of those pills from the bottle with the warning sticker showing a pair of droopy-lidded eyes."

My mad money will run out in a few days, which is also about when my johnson should fall off, so I'll be back in action shortly. In the meantime, however, should you wish to, peruse the vast transcripts being generated by Sabrina G's decision to ignore her AidSat talking earring and let the employee at the other end turn it into an open microphone.

The tape from last week even features her deflowering, with plenty of phlegmy grunting from her male partner and at least one cry of, "Keep it in!" (And what's this "Unbinding" business her colonel keeps talking about? A project of ours? And which Osmond are they referring to? I dimly remember hearing that the sister informed on a drunken third cousin of some top Saudi who'd roughed her up at an Aspen ski lodge once, but I've always thought of the brother as Mr. Clean.)

Oh, and one last favor: Kent Selkirk's got a tax problem, apparently, so let's teach him a lesson in respect and send him a hefty, alarming manila envelope with all the cultic seals and stamps of power. Delivered by a clipboard-wielding tough guy whose greeting should be: "Both sign and print your name, sir." (It's having to print it that always turns them pale.)

Off to the store now. My tramp wants Chloé sandals. She assures me that they never go on sale but she said the same thing about her Chanel purse and it was over thirty percent off. Nowadays, everyone discounts when they have to. Even smug Parisians.

I needed this break.

16.

[Via satellite]

"I have a confession, Colonel Geoff. I drove over to Kent's last night while you were sleeping. He said he wanted me to meet his dog. It yipped at me over the phone and sounded darling—one of those smallish breeds without much fur whose hearts you can see faintly beating through their skin. The ones whose thin skulls you can cover with one hand and feel their whole souls alive against your palm.

"On my way to his place, I stopped at my apartment to pay some bills and make sure my heat was off. There was something on my computer from my sister: a bunch of research I asked for about Kent that a friend of hers looked up on the Web. I couldn't understand the software program that I needed to open it and read it, though, and plus I decided that it wouldn't be right, so I dragged it to the trash. How would I like it, I mean, if somebody raided my mailbox or stole my diary and found out, oh, I don't know, about the eye doctor whom I let diddle me to get free LASIK? Sure, it's the truth, but I've changed inside since then. If people can't keep a few secrets here and there, how can they free themselves up to do things differently? They can't. They're marooned with their mistakes. If Kent's made mistakes, I don't want him to be stuck with them. I want him to know he can love me and not be perfect. Is that naive of me?"

(Unintelligible)

"That's an awfully unforgiving attitude. Take your friend Tom Cruise. Those things he did. Those people you caught him with behind the pool house. Well, now he knows better. He has a lovely baby. He deserves to move forward, to grow. To be a daddy."

(Unintelligible)

"Fine, we'll disagree. It doesn't matter. This is about me. Last night. With Kent.

"In the courtyard between our apartments there's a fishpond, and as I was heading over I threw some coins in it and made a few silly wishes about my future. While I was standing by the water, a policeman walked by with a flashlight and a pet crate, shining the beam inside the little door and making cooing sounds. Then, up above me, on a balcony, I noticed Kent in his boxers, with his shirt off, smoking a cigarette. He looked all shaky. I waved to him but he didn't seem to notice me, just flicked the butt over the railing and went inside.

"When I got up there, Kent's door was open a crack and I could see him on his couch, lying facedown and sobbing into a cushion, holding it all squished up around his face. On the floor was a spilled bowl of dog food and a chew toy. I let myself in and sat down next to him and laid a hand on his heaving, sweaty back, but it was a good five minutes before he spoke.

" 'Twist,' he kept saying. 'We tried. We did our best. We're coming back. We won't give up, I promise.'

"I made him a toaster waffle and some green tea and then sat back down and massaged him while he ate and told me that until he got the dog he hadn't known what love was, or devotion, but now he knew and was sorry that he did. He talked a lot about justice—how there was none—and admitted to me that he was bad once, irresponsible, and used to stay awake for days on drugs and hallucinate that there were trolls inside his walls writing his thoughts down and peeping through the cracks and creeping out at night to steal his T-shirts and tear them up into rags to build their nests. To stop them, he'd stab a steak knife through the Sheetrock and wiggle the blade until he heard them curse him, and then he'd shove the knife deeper until they quit.

"We ended up down on the floor together, kissing, and it was the closest I'd ever felt to anyone, and even better than our first time together. The problem was, there was dog food on the rug, and pellets of it kept sticking to Kent's damp back. When I'd roll over, they'd crunch under my hips. It was a mess. It smelled like lamb and beef. Kent's bedroom door was open across the way, and I kept begging him to take me there so we'd have a mattress and pillows to make things cozier, but he was holding on to me like death. When we were finished I looked into his eyes and I thought I could see his actual brain behind them, all gray and curled up tight and glistening. It didn't scare me, though. It reassured me. When you finally let someone in, completely, wholly, it's nice to know that he has insides, too.

"Afterward, I toasted two more waffles and we ate them with butter and jelly at his table, which was covered with dice and tarot cards that he told me he fools with sometimes when he can't sleep and feels like he might need guidance with 'inner conflicts.' We talked about whether we wanted kids someday or if we should just fly to Thailand and adopt, since the world was already overpopulated. Then Kent started crying about the dog again. He said he'd stolen it to save its life but that he'd been betrayed by someone and might never find out whom. He'd have to live without friends now, trusting no one. 'Except for me,' I told him. He shook his head. 'Including you,' he said. Then I cried, too. He stood up and went to his bedroom and shut the door and wouldn't open it for fifteen minutes, until I threatened to kick it in.

"His computer was turned on and open on his desk, and he let me lie down and watch TV while he typed in what had happened to him that night and stored it in what he called his 'archive,' where he said his words would outlive both of us. I asked him what good that would do. He said he didn't know yet. He said that what people learned from his experiences was up to them, not him.

"Then he asked me if you could get Tom Cruise's address." (Unintelligible)

17.

[DHL]

Dear Mr. Cruise,

You don't know me. You don't know most of us. I assume, though, that you imagine us sometimes. I assume that when you're in your office or in your house, protected by your alarm systems and guards, shielded by layers of bulletproof smoked glass and surrounded by video cameras and panic buttons, you occasionally find yourself picturing the faces of those whose obscurity supports your fame. The faces aren't actual faces, I suspect, but composites made up of features glimpsed in crowds. A forehead you spotted from a hotel balcony. A chin you saw through the windshield of your limousine. And though these faces disgust you, possibly, I like to think that they rouse your pity, too, because they remind you, vaguely, of your old face. Unrecognized. Unphotographed. **Unformed**.

A face that may as well be my face, now.

You're probably wondering how I found your address. I got it indirectly and dishonestly, by pretending to have feelings for a young woman who cares part-time for the retired marine who taught you to walk like a pilot in *Top Gun*. Colonel Geoff says hello to your family, by the way, and sends his regrets for missing your premiere. He isn't a well man these days, laid low by a virus that he may have gotten from you, in fact—or given to you without your knowing it. It's a puzzle, this bug. It's one of the strange new ones that's either about to break out globally or suddenly mutate into extinction.

That's not why I'm writing this, though. I need your help. I've probably needed your help for a long time, but now I finally have a way to ask for it.

Everything that I've ever considered precious, they've taken from me, Mr. Cruise. And now, this week, they're doing it again.

On Wednesday a policeman took Twist, my dog. He came for her without knocking, at suppertime, luring her into a pet crate with a Milk-Bone. It reminded me of when I was seventeen and I lost my best friend, the boy who bunked below me, who'd called in anonymous bomb threats to our boarding school. He wasn't prepared for exams—he needed time. We all needed time that semester. We were floundering. We'd come to the school with a hundred teenage maladies, from nail chewing to obesity, and we'd thought that recovering from them would be enough. But no, they demanded that we learn history, too. The names of the kings and the plots behind their deaths. The dates of the battles and the weapons that won them. My friend and I were in the dining hall, bending our forks back and flicking macaroni up into the grates that covered the lights, when the headmaster and his grim assistant appeared. They read no charges, produced no writs or warrants. They merely said, "Follow us," and my friend did. Out of the building and into a parked car that carried him down the driveway and through the gates and off to wherever they keep the things I love once it has been determined that I can't have them.

The next confiscation occurred a few years later, when I missed three payments on a leased Mustang that I should have known I couldn't afford. My only income at the time came from participating in focus groups that met in a room behind mirrored one-way glass. The job involved the tasting of new breakfast cereals and long conversations about political issues such as the food-stamp program and school prayer. I was an average citizen, supposedly, hired at random, but the truth was that the firm that sponsored the groups kept lists of people with nothing better to do, who it knew could be summoned on a few hours' notice.

I adopted a role in these groups: the stickler. If a cereal was named Blueberry Morning, I dug in my bowl for the pellets of dried fruit and complained when I counted only four of them. I objected to food stamps being used for sweets, and asked to hear the prayers recited aloud. This attitude won me steady work at first, but when I became notorious and conspicuous, the firm let me go. And then my car was snatched. The repossessors who chained it to the wrecker asked if there were personal items inside. When I answered, "Yes, I've been living in this vehicle," they laughed and powered up the winch.

And then three years ago they took my novel.

I started writing it when I heard somewhere that, by law, the Library of Congress must store and catalog any book-length work produced by an American author. This was a right of citizenship, apparently, and the only one I'd ever heard of that struck me as worthwhile. I approved of voting and free speech, and I would have defended them, I suppose, if called to, but the right to claim space for one's writings in a great building maintained by the taxpayers genuinely excited me.

I went to work immediately, composing the story during the drives between the carnivals and fairs where I demonstrated Vita-Mix blenders. My hero, named Brock in honor of my old friend, was blessed with the power to walk through solid objects. An ordinary fantasy, perhaps, but ingenious in this case because Brock's talent could be exercised only once before it vanished. So he had to choose carefully. He had to think. Should he use up his gift to save the anguished stranger who'd taken an overdose in a locked hotel room? Or should he wait to help an innocent child? But which child? And how innocent, exactly?

You can imagine the suspense. What you can't imagine, I'll wager, is the ending. Brock died undecided. He never spent his magic, which was passed along to the last person he saw (a female cashier in a hospital cafeteria) in much the same manner that it was passed to him when an old postal clerk suffered a fatal stroke while helping him fill out a money order. Indeed, as the novel ultimately revealed, this gift of immateriality had never been exploited. Instead, it had driven all of its bearers mad.

But all was not lost. In the epilogue I hinted that the cafeteria cashier would be one who at last employed the power, using it to intervene in a momentous planetary crisis whose nature I left unspecified but which I suggested related to the invention of a "cognibomb" that destroyed people's minds but left their bodies intact.

The day I finished the novel (on a typewriter bought for ten dollars from a junk store, since I couldn't afford a computer at the time), I made

five copies on acid-free stock, had them profes-
sionally bound in vinyl covers, and sent them off
by certified mail to the Library of Congress. I
didn't keep one for myself because I assumed that,
as a U.S. citizen, I'd always be able to visit the
library and read my book. When a week passed,
then two, and the package still hadn't been signed
for, I contacted an official at the library, who gave
me so little satisfaction that I telephoned my con-
gressman. I spoke to an aide who called herself Jeanine but wouldn't give me her last name. She
confirmed that my book deserved a catalog number and promised to get back to me. I waited. I
phoned again ten days later and lost my temper.

"Big libraries shouldn't screw with people," I
said. "It only takes one kitchen match."

Jeanine then asked for my Social Security number. I hung up and never called again.

The title of the book was *Portal People*, and it no
longer exists in any form.

But my dog does, somewhere, and I demand
her back.

Can you help me with any of this? Of course
you can. You've struck the deals that give people
long arms. But will you ever read this plea? I doubt
it. As I said, I obtained your address thirdhand,
through a woman I'd lied to and a man I'd met just
once, neither of whose stability I can vouch for. I
can't afford to run background checks, as you can.
I can't pry solemn pledges from my associates by

placing them under contract and on salary. I'm on my own here, drifting with the herd. All I can do is rely on foolish grace. I know that you have a new movie coming out in which you presumably save the world again. Wouldn't it be a touching publicity stunt if you could also rescue a displaced animal?

You don't know most of us. I understand that. But **we have faces**, Mr. Cruise. And though they're made up of the foreheads, cheeks, and chins that were left over after you chose your face, the day will come when our features are stripped away and dumped back into the hat for a new drawing. How will you fare then? Mathematics suggests not well. I suspect that the next round will belong to me, in fact, and that the letters begging favors will stream toward my box then.

The power resides with you now, Portal Person, but it hasn't stopped moving. It's only passing through you. That's not a threat. It's the physics of what is. I know you're a student of esoteric science, so I'm sure you get my drift.

Expecting nothing but hoping much,
Kent Selkirk

18.

[Via courier]

Agent's Memo: Returning from my vacation by the sea, my skeleton aligned, my organs cleansed, and all my buildups flushed, I decided to press on with this assignment in the manner that you, my supervisors, perennially warn against and thereby subtly recommend. First convict and then investigate. And by investigating, instigate. If the new science has it right and (as I understood it from a seminar) **to observe is to disturb**, it should also be true that to follow is to push.

But would pushing do the trick? My experience tracking Grant and Selkirk had shown me that pressuring certain people only causes them to skid in circles, like shopping carts with broken front wheels. To bring them to justice (or, rather, to determine what justice might consist of in their case) would call for a slyer maneuver. I had to **tempt** them to push back. Otherwise, they might move but never advance. They might envision but never execute.

I think it's working. I'm turning them toward evil.

Last Sunday night, alone in my apartment after breaking things off with my new crush over her contact with her ex-boyfriend—whom, I'd learned from her cell phone records, she'd kept calling even after I'd ordered her to stop— I looked up from a tray of Lean Cuisine lasagna to see a dark figure pass my curtained front window. I assumed that my brat had returned. They always do. (And I always let them, if only for an evening.) As I went to the door to check the peephole, though, my gut said trouble. I stepped back. A moment later I heard breaking glass and saw the curtain billow inward. I was en route to my bedroom and my sidearm when another pane shattered, the curtain flapped again, and a cheaply framed poster of Marilyn hanging on the opposite wall suddenly slipped cockeyed on its nail. The bright violet stain on her stomach told the story, but I wiped it with a finger to make sure.

Fluorescent water-based ammunition.

Paint.

Fired by multiple gunmen. Or that's what I concluded after inspecting the window and the curtain and finding gaudy splotches of pink and green. In the shadowy courtyard, reconstructing trajectories, I called out for Selkirk and his comrades to behave like males and show themselves. When no one came forward, I went to call in a work order to the maintenance staff. That's when I saw the words on my front door, written in orange children's sidewalk chalk.

THE WRATH OF TWIST!

He'd guessed, though it had taken a few days. He'd guessed that I'd sent the law to grab the dog that he'd confessed to abducting in his MyStory journal. I'd expected this. I'd also hoped it would start a fight.

In bed that night, out hard, I dreamed that my late wife, Jillian, had given birth to twins and hadn't, as in reality, died from a drug interaction while carrying twins. The dream was blissful, but I tried to make it heavenly by practicing the "directed wishing" trick that I'd learned from a psychic at the spa. By issuing firm commands to my subconscious, I sought to turn the imaginary babies into imaginary young adults with solid educations and stable careers. It worked, but not as smoothly as I'd hoped. Perhaps because I'd refused to learn the gender of my late wife's four-month never-borns, my invented descendants lacked definition. Dumpy, ambiguous physiques. Dull midrange voices. Collar-length blah hair. And, for clothing, identical gray jumpsuits. Worse, the twins seemed to be married to each other—miserably married. They bickered. They nitpicked. They sulked. They never kissed.

And the source of their gloom? Sterility. They longed for little ones but lacked the glands. I ordered my mind to furnish them with genitals, but when they unzipped their ugly jumpsuits there were small oval mirrors in their groins. When they thrust them together the mirrors cracked and bled. The blood was silvery, like mercury, and when it dripped it burned my children's legs.

Struggling to wake myself from this slick nightmare, which had started as a dream of resurrection, I fell out of bed for the first time since fourth grade and horribly torqued my three smallest right toes, which swelled into one indivisible bruised clump. I spiked a pint of bourbon with crushed Excedrin, hoping to endure until the morning, when I could visit a well-slept specialist, but just before dawn I opted for the ER and a groggy intern. I hopped across the courtyard toward my car, was soaked by the surge from a broken sprinkler head, and ended up resting on a bench trying to light a soggy Salem with paper matches that sizzled but wouldn't flame.

And then there they were, not thirty yards away, exiting

Selkirk's second-floor apartment and heading for a staircase whose bottom step I could reach and touch with my good foot. Grant looked tumbled and pulverized by sex, her hair a static-charged loose thatch, but Selkirk's hair was wet and combed. Just hours ago he'd played the urban guerrilla, costumed in camo and war paint, probably, but now he was dressed Caucasian-casual, like a Today's Man sales rack come to life. His banality did have a certain dazzle, though, and as he descended the stairs, I had a thought: He's the prince of the kingdom we wish we didn't live in.

I nodded first. Proactive. Very frontal. I would have stood but my knot of fractured toes might have made it a wobbly performance. And I looked scary enough seated: a grimacing, wet, Excedrin-addled smoker sporting one polished dress shoe and one soiled tube sock. Miss Grant, who sometimes passed me on the walkways and had smiled at me once or twice, faded back and let Selkirk bear the brunt of me.

"It's Rob. Hi, Rob. You're back from somewhere sunny. Incredibly reckless tan there," Selkirk said.

"My family all gets cancer anyway."

"Forewarned is forearmed. So how was Jesse? Fun?"

"Deeply. From every angle. Fore and aft."

"And Rob's an aft man. Thought so."

Quick. But meaningless. Wit can be adrenal. All animals are speedy when they're threatened. When Selkirk felt safe again, he'd slump and slow, though.

"Why such an early start today?" I asked him, though most of my attention had moved to Grant, whose meekness, wariness, or muddledness had caused her to almost dematerialize. Now *there* was a talent: auto-self-erasure.

Selkirk ignored my question. "Wounded, Rob?" He pointed at my sock.

"It's self-inflicted. Any excuse for a pop of liquid morphine. I'm only half-homo, Kent, but I'm all junkie." I chuckled to keep things light and sinister, then haltingly drew myself up on tender toes and extended a hand to Miss Invisible. "Robert Robinson," I said, because obvious fraudulence is the most ominous. "Noticed you here and there but never met you."

She replied with her name, including her dressy middle name (always the mark of a born dullard), but if she shook my hand I didn't feel it. What a magical nullity she was, odorless as aluminum even after her wee-hours screwing.

"Some jackasses fucked my apartment up last night." My diction was brutal but my tone was neutral. Nothing but the morning news.

"How?" Grant said. This meant she knew. Because, in this case, the "how" was everything.

"The usual bullshit. Stink bombs. Silly String. Burning bags of dog crap. Jars of piss."

"Ish," said Grant. Then, "Ish," again, to Selkirk. If she'd been briefed about the plan, she was feeling misled about the methods. He said paint but I said flaming excrement. It might be a day of lively phone calls.

"It's nothing worth calling the cops about," I said, "but it's certainly worth some vigilante payback. I won't hit their houses, though; I'll hit their vehicles. More personal. More perturbing. More like rape."

I hadn't met Selkirk's eyes yet, but I did now. They appeared untroubled but oddly filmy, as though he possessed those translucent inner lids that God gives to animals that swim and dive. And that's what he seemed to have done: He'd submarined.

"I need my narcotics," I said. And it was true. There's no pain worse than foot pain. Nor is there any diversion that can numb it. When the hurt comes from the bottom up, when it's agony at the root, the self-important top two-thirds of us becomes an irrelevant dead trunk.

"Too bad about your mess. That's sick," said Grant, still needling her beau, I sensed. "Hope it wasn't superhard to clean. And hope you get the shot you need. Nice meeting you. There's someone I need to cook a healthy breakfast for."

And then, with no farewell to Selkirk, no pat on the arm, no smile, no blown kiss, she set out across the courtyard for the parking lot, abandoning the winding sidewalk for a straighter route through the wet grass. She thought she was being cold and cutting, obviously, but Selkirk seemed fine with it, even a bit amused. He'd already forgotten her, but her attempted snubbing meant she'd missed it—and that she'd always miss it. Which is right where you want a woman you don't care for but periodically have use for. Until you're truly done with her, that is, and need the poor fool to believe it.

This gave me an idea. An idea that, if it worked, I might regard someday as *the* idea. To clear the way for it, however, I'd have to come clean about my last idea.

"I shouldn't have joked like that. You had every right. I fucked you. I fucked your dog. You should have used pipe bombs. Hollow points. I'm sorry. My broken toes here? Karma. Kent, forgive me."

Selkirk rigid. Selkirk seizing up. Hands in pockets, elbows straight, knees locked. Selkirk convinced that if he warms to me, if he relaxes, I'll get him with a shiv. Never trust a Robert Robinson. And I might just do it. Better safe than sorry. Selkirk adds nothing to society's plus side. Anyone with lips can man a phone bank and read out canned advice on using jumper cables and treating spider bites. In the negative column, the traumas he might cause, if he's allowed to continue, are sure to be unique.

Still, he's valuable to us. If we lose Selkirk, we lose Grant, and then the old colonel, who may be our true target, and the whole toothpick castle will fall before it's built. And just when I'm laying in the central crosspiece.

"You want the rotten truth? I took your new pet because I'm jealous, Kent. I'm not a drooling aft man, no, but I am most definitely jealous. Meeting you, reading you, dating your old girlfriend (who I'm shit-scared still loves you), I've started to wish I could be you. But I can't. I can't even get your attention on the street. I don't have a lot of friends here."

Tentatively, in a whisper, calmer now: "I ignored you or something? When? I don't remember that."

"I know you saw me waving. I whistled, too."

"Sometimes I get caught up in my thoughts. Was I in the plaza on my lunch break? I'm a basket case on my lunch breaks. I'm still buzzing from the AidSat chatter. It's like the calls just keep on coming in."

"You want the dog back? I can do that. I'm ex-ATF. I can fix things. And I'm sorry."

"You were federal once? Really?"

"Low-middle federal. That's where everyone gets stuck, though."

"I hear it's not great pay."

"It buys the beer. And believe me, you start to need the beer."

He nodded. "Burnout. That's what a lot of our calls come down to. Burnout."

"In my case, flameout."

"Huh."

"Complicated episode."

"Describe it."

"Frankly, I'm in no mood right now. My toes. I might need a shoulder there, Kent. I hate to whine. . . ."

He gave his full support. He offered to drive me. I thanked him. We reached his truck. He apologized for my window-panes. I thanked him. We shared squares of gum from a packet in his ashtray and turned on the radio and watched the sun rise. And then I made my great request.

"Would you and your girl want to go for steaks sometime with me and Jesse at the W? Next weekend, say? My treat? As one big gang? Sometimes it's isolating to be a couple. For me, I mean. It's too head-on."

He nodded, but not enthusiastically. He said the idea sounded "nice," but it depended. I said that of course it depended. It all depends. But it's best to ignore this, if possible, and try things.

"I do try things," Kent said.

"So let's get steaks."

I'd lost him, though. He'd submarined again. I sensed that he was practicing staying under and that he planned to live down there someday, with Jillian, the twins, and, eventually, me.

Men can't rage forever.

19.

[Via satellite]

"AidSat? It's Sabrina Grant. I'm calling for my Active Angel. My PIN is—"

"Executive Autoforward."

"—is 765432."

"Sabrina?"

"This is Sabrina. Is this North Platte?"

"It's Kent, Sabrina."

"Malpractice. Wrong. Unfair."

"I EAF'ed you. We need to talk. It's serious."

"This is invasion of privacy. Use a phone! And no, I will not eat ribeyes with your ex-girlfriend and Mr. Fake Name who took your runty dog. Whom you're suddenly buddies with again even though you paintballed his apartment. Or stink bombed or peed on it. What-fucking-ever."

"That's not why I EAF'ed you."

"Get off my satellite!"

"Do you understand what 'passive coverage' is? When we open the line and listen in on people in case they're in danger or unconscious? Did anyone ever go over that with you?"

"AidSat can listen to me without permission?"

"For up to an hour, and then we have to signal you. Unless there's a warrant or something. A subpoena. Let me ask you this: At any time in the last three weeks or so have you gotten the cicada tone?"

"The one that reminds you to pay your bill?"

"That one pulses. This one's very different. It starts as a mild buzzing sound, but after ten minutes, if there's no response, the pitch and the volume rise at intervals until it's impossible to wear the ear jack, and anyone in a range of fifty feet will hear it and render assistance, hopefully. Even if your vital signs look good, we assume that you're incapacitated by then. If your GPS signal is working, we also send in an emergency responder."

"I'm starting not to feel so good."

"No incredibly shrill and distracting cicada tone?"

"I think my lunch is coming up."

"When I told you about my dreams of raping Rob, were you wearing your ear jack? Think. I hope you weren't."

"It might have been on a shelf at Colonel Geoff's. I've been taking it out. It bothers me. My stomach . . ."

"Are you indoors or outdoors?"

"At the day spa. Shit . . ."

"Move to a toilet or a sink. If unable to reach a toilet or a sink, locate a suitable widemouthed receptacle. If you feel dizzy or light-headed, remain in place and kneel with head tipped forward—"

"Don't tell me how to puke! Oh, God. Oh, shit . . ."

"Relax, Sabrina. Let it come. That's good. If it feels like it wants to come again—"

"Oh, hell . . ."

"It's scary, I know. Just let it have its way. Good one. Be

sure not to aspirate the vomitus. If vomitus should lodge inside the airway, clear it with a finger. Another good one. Breathing looks normal, pulse is . . . Sabrina?"

"Guggh . . ."

"Entirely natural muscular contractions."

"It's over now. I'm emptied out, I think."

"It's best not to stand yet. Stay kneeling. Proud of you."

"Will you please, just please, please stop it, Kent? I soaked my whole station. I soaked my towels, my tweezers. What are those things? They're rice. They must swell up. I'm definitely feeling better, though."

"I'm glad. So what you're saying to me is you don't think you had your ear jack in at my place?"

"I hate you now. In whole new ways."

"Take all the time you need. My only concern was, I spoke to someone earlier, someone in Portland, in our Storage Sector, and you've been on passive coverage for a while now, kind of a pretty unprecedented long while, and after I found this out I called North Platte, and—"

"Never phone me, never visit me, never bump into me at Starbucks, and never, ever EAF me. Understand?"

"If you do think you left your ear jack at Colonel Geoff's, you might want to try to remember your conversations there. I know you've been helping with his memoirs, his Holly-wood stories, his myth-ops tales—"

"I'm tasting Mexican again."

"Forget I said that. Portland's tight. It's solid. As far as data storage, Portland's like a cross between Fort Knox and the tackle box where my father kept his *Playboys*. Laugh. That was funny. I hate it when you hate me."

"That tiny jack can hear across a room?"

"Probably not. But I meant it about Portland. It's like a bank vault locked inside a tomb shot on a rocket into a black hole. How much do you two talk about Tom Cruise? He sent me his picture. I forgot to tell you."

"I want my lady in Nebraska. Put me through to her. Then get off my satellite."

"Your Active Angel's gone, Sabrina."

"Gone on vacation? She said she had a trip planned. Czechoslovakia?"

"Hungary. That's where it happened. I'm so, so sorry."

"This is a day that needs to be all over."

"She was already bad, but in Hungary she got worse. Her linings. Her organ linings. They lost 'integrity.' They're testing all our people in North Platte in case it's airborne, or maybe fluid-borne, but so far it seems like it was only her. From what we're hearing, her husband was a hunter and the family ate a lot of game. Including rabbit, which is risky."

"Kent?"

"I'm sorry, Sabrina. AidSat's mourning, too. That wise old lady was a legend here."

"Impossible. I don't believe you. She was right here with me, in my ear. I can still hear her voice. She wasn't ill. She sounded healthier than me."

"Maybe because she knew that's what you wanted."

"Good-bye, Kent. I need to be sick again. Alone."

20.

[MyStory.com]

Steaks at the W Hotel later tonight with Rob and Jesse and Sabrina. Synchronizing busy schedules and mending tender feelings took some work, but I'm not sure I'm in the mood for other people now. And don't take offense, Rob, if you're reading this; my desire to be alone is nothing personal. I had a crazy day is all, and by the time I'm done recording it here I'll have less than three hours until dinner, which doesn't feel like enough to think things through.

The conversation happened over breakfast. Sabrina had asked a favor of me last week during one of our wee-hours, patch-things-up calls: See **Mission: Impossible III** on Friday night and meet her at the colonel's the next morning to tell him what I thought about it. As an old mentor to the movie's star, he was eager for an early review, she said. Plus, he needed some cheering up. News had come from the VA that had complicated his diagnosis. Other than latent mononucleosis, none of the viruses they'd screened for had shown up in his samples, but they had found another member of his old unit—another media liaison officer—who was complaining of difficulty swallowing, painful urination, and chronic muscle aches.

No lights were on at the colonel's when I arrived. Since

learning that Sabrina's AidSat ear jack had been piping their conversations to parties unknown for going on three weeks, they'd boycotted all electrical devices except for a battery-powered radio that stood on a shelf beside the colonel's hospital bed. It was tuned to **a national phone-in show** hosted by a vicious female psychologist who, I happened to know through AidSat gossip, sometimes called in too drunk to start her car.

"It wasn't your old friend's best movie," I told the colonel. I explained then about my long letter to Tom Cruise and the paltry signed photo he'd sent me in return—a photo that struck me as neither recent nor genuinely hand-autographed.

"Kent sent the note as a prank," Sabrina said, though she knew very well that I'd been serious. There are plenty of stories of average Americans reaching out to the rich and celebrated and receiving gratifying responses. According to family legend, my great-grandfather had written to Henry Ford himself once about a defect-plagued roadster that he'd bought with seven years of savings from his dairy route. Days later the vehicle vanished from his driveway, replaced by a newer, more luxurious model with a telegram folded on the front seat: *Because I'm concerned, sir, and because I can.*

"It's a movie that I know I saw," I said, "but that I still feel like I missed. You know how the effect of certain medicines—certain sedatives, **certain sleeping pills**—is to make you forget that you've taken them? Like that."

Colonel Geoff sucked punch through a bent straw inserted in the top of a red juice box whose sides crinkled in when it was empty. He'd turned into an ant or hummingbird, subsisting on sugar water, Sabrina said. It showed in the snowfield of dandruff on his green pillowcase and in the mottled pallor of his hands, which, after he set the juice box down, lay palms-up on his blanket as though prepared to be taken for repairs.

"The movie isn't performing well," he said. "It won't meet projections." He nodded at the radio, which was the source of all his news, presumably. So much information, so many developments, and such a small hole for them to pass through.

"I've heard that about the box office," I said.

The colonel said, "It's not just him. It's all of them. They're finally about to lose their hold on us."

"I guess that the studio's blaming piracy."

"We'll be free of them soon," the colonel said, ignoring me. "The energy they've captured will be returned. That's all it is, Kent: borrowed energy. '**Tractons**,' we called them, units of human magnetism. It was an object of study for a time there, back when we still spent money on such projects: the origins and uses of charisma." He held out his caved-in juice box to Sabrina. "More, please, dear. The Gonzo Grape this time. And bring the hot-water bottles for my hips."

As Sabrina walked off, the colonel leaned nearer to me. "You used my name?"

"In the letter? More than once."

"The maniacs forget the ones who made them."

"The fans?" I said.

"Before the fans. The fans are an epiphenomenon. They're secondary. Tell me more about the film, though."

"Which aspects?"

"All of them. Give me the whole feeling."

Uncertain about my talent as a critic, I started with the jumping problem. Whenever Cruise's character, Ethan Hunt, made one of his running leaps between two rooftops, he kicked his legs in the air as though to push himself, which didn't make sense to me as a matter of physics. Nor did the rapid scissoring of his arms help him to run any faster. It looked ridiculous. Also, Cruise's face had lost its harmony. His nostrils had shrunk and resembled two small dark seeds, while his eyes had migrated so close together that their inner corners appeared to meet at times, particularly in moments of high tension such as those that followed the villain's firing of a tiny bomb up Cruise's sinuses. I liked the idea of a miniature skull explosive, but I felt that its potential wasn't fully explored. I wished that the bomb had been in there through the whole movie.

And what, I wondered, was the "Anti-God" sealed inside the transparent canister that Cruise lost hold of on a Shanghai freeway, where it was almost crushed by passing trucks? Was it the same as the substance called Toxin Five that Cruise was briefed about before his team infiltrated the black-tie reception at the Vatican? And one last problem: Why, to enter the Vatican, did the team have to tunnel through stone walls? The year she retired from teaching Montessori, my mother had toured the Sistine Chapel and been admitted with a simple ticket.

The colonel smiled and nodded as I spoke, seeming to anticipate my criticisms and to agree with most of them. Sabrina returned, and together we raised his hips and positioned the hot-water bottles. The man's bony light-nessshocked me. He felt mummified. What substance and life still resided in his flesh was concentrated in his face, whose muscles evacuated another juice box in three ferocious sips.

"Let's play a guessing game. At any point in the story," the colonel said, "did the hero expire or appear to have expired?"

"He sure did," I said.

"At the hands of a female?" the colonel asked.

"His wife electrocuted him to defuse the microscopic brain bomb."

"But she revived him?"

"Through CPR," I said. "It was nip and tuck there for a minute, though."

"And was there, by any chance, a fallen bridge? A scene of bridge destruction?"

"A fairly long one. Hellfire missiles fired by swooping drones took out a section of a concrete causeway, and Cruise had to do his jump to cross the gap. He landed just short and hung there on the edge at first, but eventually he scrambled up."

"Was the star condescended to, at any time, by a Negro male of higher rank? By someone who roughly resembled yours truly, say?"

This one stalled me. I had to think. "On his team he had a black man, yes. Also, at the end, he asked his boss—"

"A man of color?"

"Yes. He asked him what was inside the canister that he'd spent the movie tracking down and risking his life to keep intact."

"And his Negro superior brushed off this query?"

"Totally. Which I found frustrating," I said. "Here's this supposed container of Anti-God, which may or not be the same as Toxin Five—"

"The fellow's been stripped. We've stripped him," said the colonel. He drew the straw out of the juice box and compressed it slightly at its hinge between a thumb and forefinger. "What you and the world have just witnessed, Kent," he said, releasing the straw, which sprang back straight, "is the end of an engineered event. The reversal of a major myth-op. I'd like to know who we had on this one. Danziger? It has a Danziger ring to it. Sabrina?"

"Yes, Colonel Geoff?"

"I need my stationery. There's a note of congratulations I'd like to write."

Sabrina rose. I stayed.

"Tractons," I said.

"Once concentrated, now dissipated. Take the ruptured bridge. A potent 'mytheme.' A lot like the vertical flybys in *Top Gun*, but with the opposite effect. It disperses the energies. It doesn't bind them. The mock-murder by the Delilah-wife figure, too, as well as the star's resurrection through her mercy. A man's a castrato after that. His face may still sell a few tickets, but not to women. Not Caucasian women, especially. We stripped him good and bare with this one."

"Why? May I ask why?" I said.

"Why are tall buildings demolished? To clear the lot. These performers we helped train, these mesmerists we put in place, they take up a lot of space, Kent. In the mind."

"Not in this mind."

"No? Think it over in bed tonight," he said. "Sabrina, it's my nap time. Get my mask. Can you hear me in there, dear?"

"I'm coming."

I stood to leave. The colonel touched my hand. It warmed my whole arm, somehow. The surge of tractons.

"You'll be back. Soon, I hope," he said.

"Yes, sir, I will."

"With questions."

"Probably."

"It's a set of procedures we developed. It isn't a miracle; it isn't fate. And it just happened to be him we chose. It could have been anyone with pleasing features. Even you," the colonel said.

"I know that, for some reason. I realize that."

"We wanted a role in everything. Journalism, business, academia. The entertainment world we couldn't touch, though. Politically hostile, socially impenetrable. Then we put our heads together. It's amazing what half a billion dollars and ten or fifteen PhDs could do back then."

"Tom Cruise was invented by our government?"

" 'Improved' would be more accurate. Now, apparently, we're through with him. You think I've lost my ever-loving marbles."

"No. But I feel like I need to lie down, too, now."

"We're all going to need our rest soon, with what's coming. You go lie down, boy."

And now that I've written this, **I think I will.**

21.

[Via courier]

Agent's Memo: The booth at the W faced a window that took in the busy valet-parking lot. The rich and famous were in town that night, laden with designer garment bags and zipper-cased sporting-goods equipment. The women had that **aging-ageless look**, like heavily doctored photos of themselves, and their bodies repeated the curves and cuts of the **late-model sports coupes** they stepped out of. The men were not as smoothly molded, but I could feel the excitement of the staff as it vied for the tips concealed inside their handshakes. I worked for gratuities during my college years, and it's a desperate way to live. After a while, your smiles are not your own.

Jesse, my brat, arrived for dinner first, already tipsy and argumentative but dressed in a manner that made her black mood bearable. Since our first breakup the week before, we'd undergone two more entire cycles of rupture and repair, both of them entailing costly visits to the Neiman Marcus lingerie floor. I feared that unless I made things last with her, my investments in her undergarments had grown too extensive ever to recoup. There were corsets that I might never see her wear and certain bra-and-panty combinations that her next man would gain more pleasure from than I would.

"I thought this was a double date," she said. Her first

vodka gimlet was nothing but ice by then, and her second was on its way. In the meantime, she'd made a move on my martini. "Where's Cass and his little lady?"

"He goes by Kent now."

"And next year he'll go by something else," she said. "He's still in play. Still forming. That's his charm. When we met, he called himself a Christian. Then he became a 'deep ecologist.' A couple weeks later, on his bedside table, I found a Koran. On a stack of *Penthouse Forums*. Next to a sign-up form for a tai chi class."

"Selkirk studied the Koran?"

"Is the Koran the one that Buddha wrote?"

"Not according to tradition, no."

"Then it might not have been the Koran. I don't remember. Maybe it was **The Tibetan Book of the Dead**. How much do you love the pattern in these stockings?"

"As much as I thought I would when I bought them for you. Let's go back to the mystery scripture on Selkirk's nightstand."

Jesse's gaze had slanted toward the window, where a woman with rocky little childish features set in a concave, banana-shaped face was stepping out of a silver BMW. She smiled in the manner of the oft-photographed.

"It's her. Holy shit!" said Jesse. "It's what's-her-name. That lesbian slut who broke up Grace and Chad. The couple from *The Enchantress*, season three. Who's in that commercial for Dovebars now. Malicia?"

There is no such thing as empty-headedness. All of our brains are full of what they're full of, and all of us are authorities on something. Sadly, my Jesse possessed expertise in a field that mattered only to her. This was true of Selkirk, too, who arrived a few minutes later without his date, wearing sneakers and a flag-themed tracksuit and bearing a bug-eaten bouquet of white and yellow supermarket roses.

"For you," he said, laying the flowers in front of Jesse. He stood there, apparently waiting for her to smell them, with a brilliant pink rash in the center of his throat that made him look like an agitated songbird. When our waiter approached, he ordered a neat manhattan without looking up from the flowers.

"Sit down," I said. "I'm perspiring just watching you. Where's Sabrina, Kent?"

"The hospital. Her friend Colonel Geoff had a crisis about an hour ago. As soon as my drink comes, I'm headed over there. Jesse, darling? Jesse, honey?"

"Yes?" She seemed insufficiently afraid of him. Their time as a couple, from what she'd told me, had been brief and mutually unsatisfying, and yet I detected a tolerance between them that reminded me of my parents' relationship in the last few years before my father died. They'd seen every behavior that the other one was capable of and could no longer be disappointed, hurt, startled, or angered.

"What?" said Jesse. "Tell me."

Selkirk collected his drink and tipped it back, cherry and all, into his blushing gullet. He set the glass down on the table and zipped his tracksuit top up to his chin, as though he'd suffered a chill.

"By the way, in the lobby just now," he said, losing his focus or his nerve, perhaps, "I saw that Malivia woman from that show we loved."

Jesse nodded.

"We watched too much TV, I think. We didn't talk enough," said Selkirk. "Nobody does anymore. That's going to change, though. It was a temporary imbalance, Jesse. It's all coming back to us. All that power. Soon. At AidSat tomorrow, I'm going to spread the word. I'm going to tell all my callers to prepare themselves."

"Sit, Kent," I said. An order. But he ignored it. I opened my menu and withdrew. I'd planned an evening of mischief and provocation, hoping that with enough jealousy and alcohol I could arouse in this circle of latent offenders a measure of overt hostility—toward me to begin with and, later on, perhaps, toward society at large. There were so many outrages and brutalities that I could imagine them being guilty of, but I couldn't wreak their havoc for them. I could only flush out their desire to do damage and suggest possible means for its expression.

But not tonight. I'd given up. All I wanted now was a rare ribeye.

"And when this new world comes," said Kent, "I want us to go forth in it together. Tell me you will. Say yes."

"To what?" said Jesse. "I don't know what you're saying to me, exactly."

"You will," said Selkirk. "Right now I have to run, though. I'm needed at the VA hospital. Good night, friends."

After he left us, hustling through the parking lot and up an alley between two banks, I asked my girl the question that he'd been too confused to ask, I felt, or at least too jazzed up to ask straightforwardly. I'd had three martinis by then but wasn't drunk. I asked because I liked her stockings and all the other naughty fineries I'd filled her closet with. I couldn't stand the idea that some other man might one day benefit from my lavish outlay.

Her answer: "No."

Her reasons: "Besides the fact we hardly know each other, I just don't love you. I love **someone else**."

My reaction: "Try their blackened T-bone. I hear it's a killer piece of meat."

22.

[ExpressLink.com]

Sabrina,

We fear for you, big sister. You don't reply. And you haven't acknowledged receiving the research file that my pal here at eBay assembled on Kent Selkirk. I'm guessing that you haven't read it, because if you had, you would have gotten back to me, almost certainly in tears.

So let me be the bearer of bad tidings: Not only isn't this character who he says he is, he isn't (from what I can gather) anyone.

Though there was a Kent Selkirk, once upon a time. A number of them, actually. But only one of them was white, Midwestern, and would be the same age today—were he alive—as your Ray-Banned man of mystery. This Kent Selkirk was born in 1976, the day before our nation's Bicentennial, in Thief River Falls, Minnesota. His father, Norris, owned a two-plex movie theater and headed up the local chapter of a now-defunct fraternal lodge, the Ancient Order of the Plains Astronomers, which claimed to derive its creeds and ceremonies from a Native American birchbark scroll containing the "Improved Ojibwan Star Plattes." All that's known of Kent's mother, who died when he was five, is her name, Alicia, and her gift of a sixteen-volume family scrapbook to her county historical society.

In 1993, the record shows, the first Kent Selkirk took seventh place in a regional essay contest backed by the National Rifle Association ("Self-Defense: A Common Good") and was cited, twice in the same month, for operating a motor vehicle while under the influence of a scheduled substance. He enrolled one year later at Cass Academy, a military school in Minneapolis, from which he was later expelled for unknown reasons. After a misdemeanor marijuana arrest and a charge, later dropped, of sending threatening letters to the faded pop sensation Boy George, he joined the coast guard, was stationed in Sitka, Alaska, and died in the crash of a Sea King helicopter in February 1997 while evacuating a capsized Russian crab boat.

According to his recent writings on MyStory .com, the fraudulent composite who has since adopted Selkirk's name also grew up in Minnesota and also attended Cass Academy. But according to a range of documents—some publicly available, many not, and a few of the most sensitive obtained through anonymous channels at Dad's law firm— he shares little else with the original Selkirk, whose Social Security number he started using in the fall of 1999, first to obtain a Montana nonresident hunting license and then to complete an employment application for a "VIP personal security" post at Proton Protective Services of Chicago. The outfit fired him twenty-four days later for "violating professional decorum" while guarding the greenroom of *The Oprah Winfrey Show.* This pseudo-Selkirk, according to our data, is five inches taller than his namesake, blue-eyed not brown-eyed, sandy-haired not blond, and possessed of a nineteen-point IQ advantage that classifies him as a "low-mid near-genius."

I've also seen and compared the two men's photographs. In a CyberCupid online dating profile from 2001, your fellow posted a series of color snapshots (crudely and unconvincingly Photoshopped) depicting him in a poncho and Nike baseball cleats standing atop what he refers to as "the Six Sister Peaks of Old Bhutan." This faux alpinist doesn't resemble in the slightest the Selkirk in Cass's sophomore memory book, who is shown accepting a framed citation for excellence in night reconnaissance. He does share, however, the X-creased forehead of another Cass student named

Ormand Dorngren, who, after reneging on a commitment to army ROTC, went on to study dramatic arts at Furley Junior College in Spokane, Washington, but left after two semesters to play a seraph in South Dakota's Black Hills Passion Play.

Dorngren, too, is dead, however. In the spring of 2001, during an Earth Liberation Front assault on a salmon-killing Canadian dam, he was sucked underwater by massive turbines that presumably pulverized his body, which was never recovered. Oddly, a picture that ran with the obituary in his hometown Minnesota newspaper shows a young man much leaner and sharper-featured than the sweet soldier boy of the memory book or the phony outdoorsman on CyberCupid. I can only suppose that Dorngren, the former acting student, enjoyed experimenting with his appearance, much as neo-Selkirk likes tinkering with digital-imaging software.

For the last six years or so, your "Kent" (who also goes by the first names KC and Casey) has made his presence felt on numerous Web forums related to a dumbfounding array of hobbies, issues, and enthusiasms. In 2000, for example, he joined an international petition drive urging the People's Republic of China to release imprisoned practitioners of the outlawed martial art Qigong. At about the same time, on CyberCupid, he revised his description of his ideal date from "Picnicking on blueberries and wine as our dogs chase Frisbees through the wildflowers" to "Getting sweaty in my Dodge while blasting classic Pantera tracks." Two months later, on another dating site intended for under-thirty faithful Mormons, he described his profession as "touring antigang speaker" and summed up his personal philosophy as "Always taking care to close the carton and leave at least one glassful for the next guy." The book that he said had most influenced his life? The *Rand McNally World Atlas.* "It reminds us that we're surrounded by H_2O, almost all of it undrinkable and much of it in the form of ice. Kind of humbles you and makes you wonder."

This, big sister, is only the beginning of your quasi-Kent's electronic odyssey. Other high points include a hysterical nine-page e-mail to the respected blogger Andrew Sullivan, in which he contends that "loose American college girls spreading drug-resistant STDs across the spring-break beaches of the globe" justify "anything Islam can throw at us but especially the bio-stuff." Two years later, here on eBay, he ran a short-lived enterprise selling "ionized wild sheep colostrum" as a therapy for childhood autism, which he hinted that he'd suffered and recovered from.

Just weeks after we shut him down, he popped back up as a source for "Egyptian EroSalt," a powdered aphrodisiac for women that he boasted was capable of turning "a slumbering menopausal nun" into a "nymphazoid all-night bedpost humper."

Meanwhile, over on NasaKnows.com, a site devoted to the search for extraterrestrial life, he claimed that concealed in the SimCity computer game is a video clip of Billy Graham, Muhammad Ali, the Bush brothers, and others bowing to what he calls "the Orionic Eminence" on a dry lakebed in the Utah desert. On a site for cosmic rationalists, SaucerScoffers.net, he mocks the same notion as an urban legend.

I think you get the picture. There is no picture. Whatever his parents really named him and his teachers brought him up to be, "Kent Selkirk" has shed his mortal form to become **a holographic data-ghost** composed of appropriated biographies and incompatible sensibilities. Stay away from this goon. If you're with him now, get out. If he follows you, fire at his midabdomen and, once you're certain the beast is down, call Dad.

Even though no further warnings should be needed, I leave you with this excerpt from a short bio that KS submitted just ten months ago to a matchmaking service called E-Symmetry. It's headlined "Am I the One You Seek?" and it runs alongside a county-fair gag photo of the monster's toothy mug grinning through an oval hole in the head of a life-size cardboard Dalai Lama.

". . . but chiefly because my vocation is compassion. Eight hours a day, five days a week, I don a satellite-connected headset into which my far-flung fellow humans funnel their confusion and apprehension. Sometimes the work exhausts me, I'll confess, but not once in my years of assisting faceless strangers have I forgotten to whom I'm truly listening: traumatized newborns, whose lifelines have been severed, forcing them to solicit sustenance by wailing and shrieking nonstop until they die."

Please don't kiss this creature. Please don't touch him. Remember when I was six and you were eight and we emptied a packet of dehydrated brine shrimp into a mayonnaise jar full of water? Remember how those tiny, eyeless swimmers fluttered translucently to life and survived in the fluid untended and unfed until it evaporated and we replaced it—only to watch our "sea monkeys" revive themselves? This is the sort of being I fear you're dealing with, but a million times larger, posing as a man.

Hugs abounding,
Your sleepless little sister

23.

[MyStory.com]

The access code I've added to this page should frustrate all trespassers, including Rob, who's become a pest these last few days despite having made good on his promise to work through his old connections in law enforcement and have my precious Twist returned to me by county animal control. She spent a good part of this evening in my lap, her nose shoveled into the pocket in my shorts, where there must have been some crumbs left over from the torn package of Zingers that I bought in the VA hospital vending nook and ate for supper at Colonel Geoff's bedside here. With Sabrina checked into her facility (so much to tell, and no best order to tell it in), I'm the old soldier's nighttime sitter now. His CAT scans came back normal and, medically speaking, he's regained consciousness, but until tonight it wasn't a productive sort of consciousness—more like the shuddering nap of a male lion nagged by biting flies.

As the IV line leaked sustaining syrup into the Band-Aided crook of his left arm, and the nurses came and went with the humdrum sterile items whose noisy unwrapping and disposal drag out the drowsy hours in a hospital, I scritch-scratched the little bumps under Twist's fur and tanned my uptilted face in the flat light of TV shows about the *Titanic* and celebrity plastic surgeries. Every twenty minutes, just about, the colonel would rub his dry lips with a dry hand. A moment or two before he stirred, Twist would stiffen her ears, as though registering his rising will. If she yawned as well, unfurling her slender bubblegum-colored tongue, it meant he was about to speak. I'd open my spiral notebook, mute the set, and turn into a reporter on a story that may not be true but feels important anyhow.

"She'll shed half her tractons during this new concert tour. That's the next big wave of them." The colonel was referring to Madonna, who'd been on TV while I was eating Zingers, plushly backgrounded by her London parlor and praising herself for her kabbalah studies. "The minute the woman's sufficiently demagnetized, people will see her as she is," he said. "Just a very muscular aging rich lady, all bristle and snap and anger at her staff, and stuffed with so much pushy mystic bullshit that we might have to Taser her to back her off."

"The nurse left butterscotch pudding if you want some. Or just the whipped topping with the chunk of pineapple? It's time to go back to solids," I said.

"Where's Sabrina?"

"Resting. On a break." The facts but not the truth.

The truth had to do with a scalpel she'd found somewhere and stealthily poked through the side of my white sweatshirt while we were eating ice cream with Rob and Jesse in the hospital cafeteria four nights ago. This merry social, Rob's idea, was meant to make up for the steaks we'd never had, but he seemed to be driving at something wicked from the moment we lined up at the sundae bar. While the girls were spooning up chopped pecans, he asked me if I'd read or heard about "this huge new phone records scandal in D.C." I said that I had but didn't understand it or know quite why it should bother me personally. "Do widespread violations of civil liberties have to bother you personally?" Rob said, squirting a black puddle of Hershey's syrup into the bottom of his empty bowl, then plopping three scoops of mint chip on top of it.

"That's backward. That's upside-down," I said.

"You know what isn't, Kent? Striking back before they snatch it all. First our phone calls, then our letters, and on and on until their filthy fingers are six inches deep inside our girl-friends' VJs, taking test-smears of our semen. But hey, don't take it personally, Kent."

"I won't."

"Kent. Kent Selkirk. Of Seven Decorah Drive. Who rerented *Aguirre, the Wrath of God* last week, as well as *Scarface, Finding Nemo, Bruce Almighty*, and *The Parent Trap*. The fat retard clerk there? Photographic memory. I bribed him with a box of Goobers peanuts."

"Why?"

"Because it's possible."

"Okay."

"Feel violated?"

"Nope."

"Then there goes the Constitution."

"Fine," I said.

In the half hour before Sabrina stabbed me, the talk at our table slid around like a pumpkin seed on a greased platter. I'd think that I was advancing some theme or topic—the sadism behind the concept of purebred dogs, whether Jesse ought to go lighter with dark streaks, why I believe we'd have less domestic violence if men could just say, "I divorce thee," like the Muslims do—but when an idea rebounded off Rob, it came back as something political and harsh or something personal and even harsher. Did we know there were lists on public Web sites of women who have prescriptions for the abortion pill? Had we heard that in certain impoverished arid nations Coca-Cola had suctioned dry the water table to supply its bottling plants? And what was it with me and my fondness for small dogs? If Rob had a dog it would be a German shepherd, male, unfixed, with combat training. So he could sic it on "that pig Scalia," whom he described to Sabrina, to bring her in on things, "as the wizard-*consigliere*-grand inquisitor of the new Orwellian white reich."

It irked me that Jesse let him steam this way without nudging my foot under the table or joining me in my sighs. We had a history; she and Rob had spending sprees. We had chemistry; they had latex sex toys. Destiny longed for us to mate and breed but would just as soon see Rob die childless in a Reno strip-club parking lot.

I didn't feel the prick, the stick, the slice. What they say about scalpels proved accurate. Perhaps because I didn't flinch, Sabrina wondered if she'd really punctured me, which may have been why she withdrew the weapon, studied it—in the open, with everybody watching her, though still unaware that its blade had been inside me—and then reorganized, stared at me, and said, "Whoever you are, I bet you fucking bleed, though you didn't the first time, so let's try again."

Once a man is sure that its thin steel is headed for the fat grape of his right eye, a scalpel in a woman's hand is an easy object to gain control of. And once three bored old veterans of foreign wars have spotted what may be their final chance to charge in low and fast, that woman's body will smack the floor so hard that ice-cream spoons will rattle in their bowls.

"When's she coming back?" asked Colonel Geoff. "Do I smell dog in here?"

"And dog smells you. Happy, twitching, dilated wet nose. You want her on the bed? I bet she'll stay. Here, I'm doing it. Under your IV arm. They say now that snuggling a pet can speed recovery."

The colonel closed one of Twist's ears in a loose fist and smoothly stroked it from base to tip. Again. Again. Intent on taking therapy. We watched more TV and he told me that indeed he felt much, much better, and that in fact most folks were feeling better due to the fresh streams of liberated tractons that were spreading across the land, presumably mostly from the west.

"Sabrina cracked up. She's taking a rest at a center," I said. The colonel seemed hardy enough to take things straight now. "It's in the woods, on a big lake. I hear that it's one of those centers that doesn't seem like one. Lots of hiking and horseshoes. Healthy salads."

The colonel grunted and patted Twist, who'd rolled over on her back. I was considering giving her to him. I worked all day, and she peed when she got lonesome.

"When the Unbinding comes," the colonel said, "half of those nut bins will empty out right quick. The ones whose patients aren't critical, especially. Rich fathers can spend their money on boats again instead of talking cures for bratty kids. Momentous summer coming. The next one, more so. We're going to see quarter-billion-dollar movies shred away in the breeze like Kleenex tissues. Celluloid beauties you never thought you'd meet will ring up your pickles at the delicatessen. Captains of industry coaching girls' Little League. Crows in the rafters of the auditoriums."

"That's the Unbinding? Bad box office and so on?"

"No. Just the signs that will herald it," he said.

"Try the butterscotch pudding."

"Noxious glop. These old-time desserts that you only get in hospitals are how they shoo you toward the tomb. Who checked my girl into the booby hatch? Were the authorities involved?"

"Rob Robinson handled that," I said.

"Who in Adam's army is Rob Robinson?"

It took me a while to construct an answer. I realized I'd never asked myself this question, perhaps because it's not a question that I like people whom I meet casually and have no intention of marrying, lending money to, or marching into battle with to ask themselves concerning me. Calling cards. Introductions. Coats of arms. That old society is gone. Our new way is to show up out of nowhere, crack a joke, laugh at a joke, and then slip off again, hoping we've left a nice enough impression to assure a smile if we come back. Sweet and easy. Economical. And nothing wrong with it, I feel, considering what I've seen happen to certain people who've stood in place too long, letting their fuckups and oopses and late payments ice up around them and trap them in blocks of frost. Back at Cass, that was our teachers' great, dark threat: "*You do that one more time, son, it's going on **your permanent record**.*"

"Rob's just a guy. From around. You know. Like me." Accurate but bodiless. "He works out at my gym. He wall-climbs." Not quite there yet. "He's in telecom. Drives a silver Civic. A Republican, maybe, who's changing into a Democrat."

There. I'd done my best.

But the colonel had moved on. He was using a thumbnail to nick brown tartar from one of Twist's front teeth. Their love had quickly grown exclusive. It was almost eleven and I had work tomorrow—a redubbing session for the radio ad featuring the toaster-oven blaze that I'd helped smother from hundreds of miles away—but I doubted that dogs were allowed to spend the night here without their owners. This meant I'd have to stay; I couldn't separate the newlyweds. I kicked out the footrest on my lounger and tugged on the handle that let me flop back flat. The toes of my white-socked feet framed the TV screen.

"Seen this one ever?" the colonel said.

"What is it?"

"Rock Hudson's best. A Frankenheimer picture. Martin Balsam. Will Geer, if I recall. And some actress I'm thinking I screwed when she was older, after she'd had her bitter lesbian years. Can't be sure, though. They haven't shown her yet."

"What's the plot?" I asked.

"Middle-aged **Martin Balsam** pays ancient Will Geer to turn him into young **Rock Hudson**. He moves to a flashy California beach pad, paints abstract pictures, drinks wine, gets stoned, gets laid, then goes back to his wife in the East for some damn reason and mopes around because she doesn't recognize him. Far-fetched, I know. It's science fiction. Forgotten the title. *Second Helpings*? Someone dies, though. Guess."

"Unless it's Rock Hudson, who gives a rip," I said.

"He bleeds out on the operating table. Trying to change back into Martin Balsam."

"Why?"

"People can't stand perfection, supposedly. We crave familiarity. Baloney. We want them both, or nothing. Then again, the real Rock, who I knew some—I drilled him on antiaircraft gunnery in a wooden Warner Brothers flop—

wasn't enormously thrilled to be himself. You want your pooch back on your lap?"

"Keep her. Think of her as yours now."

Twist appeared to hear this, and looked relieved. She arched her neck to present her chin for tickling, and her right rear leg shook when she got some. I'd had her once, lost her, had her briefly again, and now I'd given her away. Missing her was all I knew of her—a relationship that had its beauty, but not the beauty of the bond she'd found with the colonel. They'd fused. They'd merged their tractons.

"When the big people lose their mystique, their power," I asked, "how do the rest of us absorb it? Through what portals, I mean? Our lungs? Our noses?"

"It's a metaphor. Don't be a dunce."

"Then how do we do it metaphorically?"

"**Tractons flow in through the skin,**" the colonel said.

I shut my eyes, tuned out the movie sounds, and tried to envision these fanciful charged particles, but I was jostled by my buzzing phone, whose jealous micromind, I'd grown convinced, had trained itself to detect me meditating. I reached into my pants to throttle the intruder, and only when the colonel had nodded off, Rock Hudson had passed away, and a nurse had crept through with a needle and a gauze pad to rustlingly unwrap and crisply discard, did I open the nasty gadget to hear who'd called.

"It's Rob. No message. Simply checking in. Just watching the news and wanting to demolish stuff and wondering if you do too sometimes. Whatever, though. I guess that you're not there."

It infuriates me when people say that. They know I'm here—there's nowhere else for me to be.

"Twist," I whispered. I patted the arm of my lounger. "Come, Twist. Come."

But no one was answering anyone tonight, and I was not her master anymore.

24.

[Via courier]

Agent's Memo: She's gone to a place where I can't follow her: The head farm. The wack house. The kookatorium. This development is frustrating in some ways, since her keepers have cached her phone and banned her laptop, but, overall, I consider it a win. Our civilization still teeters on the brink, but the brink is not as loose and crumbly—and there's one fewer distracted driver on the roads.

The name of the place is the Center for New Integrity, and for just under $23,000 a month, not including charges for art supplies and personal sporting-goods equipment, it promises to help its inmates (whom its creamy vellum brochure calls "Formatives") watercolor and canoe their way back to whatever passes these days for sanity (which the brochure calls "EmoPoise"). Her father, the bluestocking shyster, will foot the bill. Indeed, he's already wired off the cash for princess's first eight weeks of EmoFormatting. (Blue Cross refused to pay, probably after skimming the brochure, which is lavishly illustrated with patient "art" of the butter-fly-over-a-rainbow-inside-a-moon-which-forms-the-eye-of-a-coiled-serpent school.)

Because the center's forested perimeter is gated, fenced, video-cammed, and possibly mined, and also because the nearby gravel roads are haunted by a suspiciously large number of domestic four-door sedans driven by broad-shouldered chain-smokers in windbreakers, I expect that the current class of Formatives includes at least one or two daft British royals, the normal cohort of garbled Kennedys, several hallucinating Saudis, and maybe even a manic Bush-by-marriage. If single Miss Grant is scouting for a rich groom now that Selkirk has turned toad on her, she's dancing at the right cotillion. I just hope the marriage yields no offspring. Cross that anorexic Yankee blood of hers with the warlord chromosomes of a Salvadoran plantation heir or the flyaway genes of a young Welsh viscount, and we'll need **a new monkey house for the human zoo**.

I just wish I could get inside the place. Yesterday afternoon I walked its fence lines, summoning all my cunning to simulate the carefree gait of the average male, middle-aged wild-flower picker who's somehow forgotten to change out of his dress shoes or take the black ballpoint pen out of his vest pocket. I peered toward the sanctuary's built-up middle. I strained. I squinted. But all I could see through the pines were yet more pines, arrayed in those staggered, tree farm–style rows that diagonally lure away the gaze. It's **the infinity pattern of the tombstones in national ceme-teries**, and not by accident, I'm sure, because it's so hypnotic. I know it worked in my case. A school trip to Arlington. I'm seventeen. No big patriot, just a beerhead party guy. My dad says the army doles out money for college, but I'd rather be a deejay or a ski coach. And then I step off the bus and see them all.

"Come along into history," they chant. "Follow us away. Follow us all the way, down into the dirt."

Or, as it turned out, into the pinelands around a snazzy goonhouse, where I'm standing in mud-crusted brown oxfords holding a bunch of wilting bluebells when up revs a rent-a-cop on a Suzuki asking if I have a legitimate reason to be there.

"Legitimate? *Nyet. Nein.* No," I say. Staring into the depths of offset trees and wondering what exactly I found so dazzling about that vast, white, geometric graveyard.

The money for college helped but wasn't what did it.

But I do have a bit of good news, too. The Center for New Integrity, despite its fortified isolation, leaks. Twice a week it tosses a bursting Cinch-Sack of surplus patient dreamwork—hectic sketches, glum haikus, lumpy ceramics, occult collages—into the bed of a Dodge Ram pickup that carts the crap out the gate to a green Dumpster whose locked chain-link fence is missing the key fourth side that would make it a barrier, not just a screen.

So here you go, the jewel from my first haul: a poem by our favorite protosaboteur—who may never be charged but shall surely be oft detained, and perpetually sedated—that was initially written in silver glitter marker on mauve construction paper, but which I've typed out because the paper was wet. I've also repunctuated the verse, since I think it works best as one cascading sentence rather than a stack of fragments with both a period and a dash at the end of every line break, as "S. M. Grant" originally styled it.

PORTION CONTROL

Level by level, meat by meat,
Crab leg, chicken finger, eye of sirloin,
The pyramid rises to its protein peak,
While down its fruit-and-vegetable sides,
Its sloping apricot and broccoli sides,
Over its sturdy base of grains and cereals,
Stream the blood and oil
That darkly fill the broad Lake Michigan
Where I must swim behind my father's
Chris-Craft
Before school, after school, for one full hour,
Commanded to slim down
For summer balls

We've drilled a shaft into her cortex now. Those phone taps were a silly waste.

(Next week I hope to scavenge a nice pastel.)

25.

[kentselkirk@gmail.com]

Dear "Kent,"

I am all for "reinventing" oneself, but I am almost certain you are, or were, the earnest narcissist I spent a wearying evening with a year or so back. Am I right in thinking I know you? Does a little French place in the East Village after the gory Korean film at the Sunshine help?

I pride myself on being a game gal. But your colleagues and admirers should know that you are not always the aboveboard fellow you would have us believe. You did tell me—though not until the *tarte tatin* had come—that you were still very much involved with your ex. Remember what you asked me after telling me that? Remember you said, "What does that have to do with us?" I remember that I told you I would not see you again, that this hurt me, and I remember you told me not to be hurt. Remember that I then posed a multiple-choice question? I believe I said, "Kent Selkirk: A woman comes to see you in your apartment and says she is freezing. You a) get her a warm sweater from your closet, b) turn up the thermostat, c) build a toasty fire in the fireplace, or d) tell her not to be cold."

Okay, maybe you are Kent, not "Kent." But in the spirit of due diligence I feel I had to send this e-mail.

Yours,
Amy Hempel

[kentselkirk@gmail.com]

Hey, Blake. Is this you? I was looking through old camp pictures the other day and I started to wonder how you were doing. It's been forever. By the way, this is Logan, Scout Camp 1994; I know you will remember me if this is actually you. Two words for you: Team Biatchica, remember? and all the scout leaders thought it was an Italian word, ha ha! And the cow dung we put in Elias and David's tent? Do you remember all that crazy stuff we did at camp?

Anyway, I found what I thought was you on MyStory.com; at first I wasn't sure because the name said Kent, but once I got to the paintball stuff I knew it had to be you. I've been reading along with your exploits; are you okay? What's all this talk about magnetism and celebrities? You really have finally taken the plunge, haven't you. You went nutso on us, ha ha! Sounds like you are up to some crazy stuff again. Unfortunately your MyStory profile was changed to "private" the other day and I couldn't access it. Luckily I found you again online and there were pictures this time. You look a little different but mostly the same ol' Blake.

Holler at me if this is you. I miss those talks we had when you visited me in D.C. Hit me up when you get a chance.

Logan

P.S. If you check out **my porch account** you'll see a picture of us when we visited the White House. I really do look like a young Drew Carey, don't I?!

[kentselkirk@gmail.com]

Kent,

This is the last e-mail I'll be writing you. I thought we were friends, and I have given you so many chances to apologize for your actions. What you did to me was unacceptable, and I tried to give you a chance to apologize. You never did. Then the way you treated my sister is just unforgivable. Still, I gave you a chance to explain yourself and apologize once again. The only response I ever got was that fucking voice mail from when you called me drunk and started yelling and cursing at me. So now our friendship is over. I don't know how we became friends in college; you were an insecure asshole even back then. I should have known. Please don't call, write, or attempt to contact me ever again.

Brandon

P.S. If I ever hear about you trying to talk to my sister again you'll need more than your paintball gun to protect yourself.

[kentselkirk@gmail.com]

Hey there, "Active Angel."

It's Sarah Flick from Wisconsin. Remember me?

How could you? We spoke, but you never saw my face. I'm a nurse and a kidnapping victim. That ring a bell? My crankhead ex-boyfriend drugged me, duct-taped me, and drove me to California a couple of months ago—and you, I found out with a teensy bit of research (thanks to MyStory.com), were the operator who sent the cops who finally put Marcus (my ex) in the high-security lockup where he belongs (and which he'd just been released from when I started e-mailing him, which was a *major* mistake, I realized later).

I never forget a favor. Write me back, Kent.
Maybe we could meet up "in the flesh" someday.
I just hope this isn't another *huge* mistake!

Sarah Flick

26.

[MyStory.com]

Despite all the junk mail it's starting to attract from crackjobs
whom I'm not sure I want to hear from and who may believe

they know me but really don't (so please stop spamming and harassing me—except for you, of course, slinky Sarah Flick, whom I'll write back to ASAP!), I'm reopening my MyStory page and even sharing the password to my g-mail ("posies") because I want the whole world to hear my news (and especially you, Rob, over at Vectonal, which won't catch up with AidSat during this century, because you have neither the testes nor the technology).

So gather 'round, my far-flung global friends:

They've asked me to be **a corporate persona**!

It happened today at AidSat's recording studio, where our new vice president of marketing took me aside in a hallway near the elevators following my redubbing of the radio spot about the New Hampshire toaster-oven mishap. He shook my hand so hard he popped a knuckle, then fixed me with both emerald contacts and began:

"According to a multiaxis, three-million-dollar, four-month study, Kent, the American consumer—particularly the American consumer with at least two years of college—perceives our company as remote and sexless."

"How does sex figure in?" I said. "That's dumb. No wonder the world's almost had it with our culture."

"It's part of the brand's penumbra."

"Oh, yeah, that." I rolled my eyes, still feeling cocky from my grand last take of the commercial's partially reenacted call: *That mac and cheese in your oven is mostly oil. Oil burns hot. It also repels liquid. That pitcher of water is useless. Try baking soda.*

The VP of marketing went on: "Robotic and sterile also. That's not optimal. But here in the studio this afternoon I think we may have found our human voice."

I pointed two index fingers at my chest as the VP of marketing beamed appreciation. His name is Miguel Veracruz. I'd heard him slandered around the office as an unqualified diversity hire who washed out at **OnStar** after just five years, but suddenly he was now my patron, and I liked him. I liked how he squeezed my left shoulder with the Spock grip and didn't let go until I winced.

"GM brought things home with Mr. Goodwrench, Kent. I'm thinking that AidSat might bring things home with you."

"As a character or as me?" I asked.

"You *are* a character. We all are, Kent. That's the whole basis of **the new psychology**."

"I mean like Betty Crocker. Invented. Fictional."

"Based on the true Kent Selkirk and drawn from him, but heightened and broadened. 'UltraKent.' But not some ham actor. An authentic AidSat operator. What's your middle initial?"

"O. Ormand."

"KOS chimes with SOS. Intriguing."

"If we changed my first name to Skip or Stone," I offered, "it would come out as SOS exactly."

"You'd adopt a new first initial for this campaign?"

"I might consider it, sir. 'What's in a name?' and so on."

"A reputation. A lifetime of accumulated personhood."

"Besides that. Joked Kent Selkirk."

"That's all there is." The VP of marketing blammed me with a frown that showed he was more than a token Nicaraguan; he was possessed of abundant managerial tractons. "I'm lunching with our new ad people on Friday. I'll toss some ideas out; we'll see what flies, what dies, and maybe in a week or two we'll coach-class you out to Seattle for a meeting. We're contemplating the Space Needle."

"How so?"

"It's an aging icon. A dated pinnacle. We see it as ripe for renaming and relicensing. 'SliverSat.' 'SatMast.' Veracruz ad-libbing here."

"SkyKent? CloudKirk?"

"AidPeak, maybe. SatPoint."

"Does Mr. Goodwrench have a costume? The Maytag Repairman definitely has one. Would my guy wear a costume?"

"Would he like to?"

"I don't rightly know. I'll buzz him on the KentPhone. 'UltraKent . . . '?"

"Anyway, son, don't crap your khakis if I call you later on next week. Magnificent voice work this morning. A star is born."

"Or a born star is finally recognized."

"Quipped Kent."

"Will you contact me at the office or at my home, sir? I'll give you my unlisted number."

"Why unlisted?"

"Wild guess," I said.

"Most wild guesses are wildly wrong, I've learned. Prudent businesspeople avoid them."

"Women."

"Well, I'm glad it's just that."

"And American Express."

"At least you qualify for one of those."

"They *told* me I did. Not so much, it's turning out. I'm more a low-limit Discover Card type."

The VP of marketing closed his eyes in thought. "Veracruz improvising again. If our 'UltraKent' wore a cape and tights, say, and if he was clearly on wires as he flew—a dinner-theater Peter Pan effect, with maybe a *Sputnik*ish fake satellite zapping his headset with cartoon lightning bolts representing cries for help—it might have a sort of campy, retro charm along the lines of the Taco Bell Chihuahua. It's a tricky aesthetic for a large tech firm, but it certainly neutralizes 'sterile' and maybe it turns 'robotic' to goofy advantage. Though it might be a job for Claymation. Or for puppets."

"I don't think I follow."

"If we animate."

"But you have *me*," I said. "Why animate?"

The VP was backing toward an elevator whose doors his assistant had been keeping open by holding one hand across the sensor ray.

"I'll be in touch," the VP said.

"And vice-a-versa."

"No vice-a-versa, Kent. From me to you." His management tractons swept over me again, raising the frizzy hairs inside my thighs. "And please have your boss overnight me your HR files. I'll need to review them. To start the vetting process."

"Why?" I said.

"We're conjoined. You're in our ad now." He laced his fingers together and squeezed them pale.

"How long does this **vetting process** normally take?" I asked.

"That depends on what's in your HR files. Not long, I hope. I'm anxious to air this spot."

"And the countless hundreds that will follow."

"An optimist. You've read *The Seven Habits*."

"I *am The Seven Habits. Sí, señor*. Now—"

"I'm late for my flight. Just overnight those files."

The VP of marketing smiled and thumbs-upped me, took a tiny, blind step back, and his silent assistant lowered his right hand, allowing the elevator doors to shut and the lighted numbers just above them to start counting down from thirty-two to one. They stopped changing at ten, though, which puzzled me. Cabs to the airport don't wait on the tenth floor—though harried bigwigs do tell white lies sometimes when it's the lunch hour and they're growing peckish.

If AidSat's human resources department didn't share the tenth floor with the executive dining room, I would have felt more comfortable, however.

Tonight, after writing Sabrina a get-well card at the Center for New Integrity (*You watch—your troubles will all come down to serotonin levels, the way they did with me a few years back, when I shocked the Iowa state fair by threatening to stick a pinkie finger into a Vita-Mix blender I was demonstrating*) and deleting several nuisance g-mails (including one with a MySpace link I clicked on that brought up the page of some bozo, "The Living Bubba," who may or may not have hazed me once at scout camp by filling my Adidases with pickerel guts), I sat up in bed reflecting on my prospects as the Ronald McDonald of satellite assistance. Whatever they ultimately renamed the Space Needle, its antenna would make a sweet "base camp," I decided. And wearing a costume would be fine, I felt, as long as I could consult on its design. No cape, though. No tights. And no comic-book lightning bolts.

I'm not a defenseless Seattle skyscraper. I'm Kent Selkirk. A man.

I have my dignity.

27.
[Via courier]

Agent's Memo: Art from the bughouse garbage can, as promised.

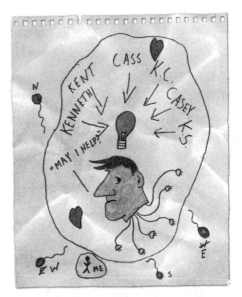

28.

[kentselkirk@gmail.com]

Dear "Kent,"

I was not surprised to hear that you remember our evening differently than I do. And btw? Just because a person asks you to park closer to the curb does not mean she has OCD.

I wouldn't write again except that a coincidence compels me. My friend Kathy thinks you are the guy who "fixed" her heater. She said you came up to her apartment for a drink and offered to get the heater going. She said you hauled in and, after a while, said, "Next, we'll throw out the lifter pump. That's one piece of hardware you don't need." My friend Kathy said she just knew those were going to be famous last words. And in fact, the next night she gave a dinner party, and her guests had to keep their coats on during dinner. Was it Kate Millett who said women need the kind of confidence men have when they don't know what they're doing?

Yours, Amy

[kentselkirk@gmail.com]

Dear Amy,

Obviously, "I'm horrifically ashamed and sometimes think I deserve to get gangrene for how poorly I treated you that night" wasn't quite enough. Nor was assuring you that I've changed since Greyhounding out of New York that humid June—partly due to your wonderful friend Kathy, the so-called "Post-it note heiress of Eighty-third Street" who, if there's any justice on this earth, is known nowadays as the Body Odor Queen of the Coney Island Subway Platform. Yes, I pretended to fix her heater once (who's Kate Millett, anyway? One of your high-chinned lady writer pals?), but I don't think that justifies how she lied about me just as I was beginning to connect with folks.

One nauseated morning-after at Kathy's Hamptons "cottage"—which looked like a mansion to my small-town eyes, and which I later discovered didn't belong to her but to a hush-hush mistress of Martha Stewart's whom Kathy knew from a New Hampshire fat farm—she accused me of having date-rape-drugged her daiquiri at a beach party the night before. The truth was she'd taken a fistful of Mexican Vicodins bought from an elderly man in white suede hot pants who was also selling turquoise glow sticks. I should have known the party would be trouble when everyone said Billy

Joel had left just fifteen minutes before we got there. I'd only been in town for seven months, but I'd already heard enough to realize that BJ exits a shindig early only if it harbors the very lowest elements.

I suppose it was easier for Kathy to slander me—a friendless young bike messenger from out of town who'd delivered a couple of envelopes to *Vogue* once but hadn't been allowed inside its offices—than to admit to her parents and the docs at the ER that the foreign object lodged inside her had not only been inserted at her direction but lubricated by her own left hand. In the end, that's what chapped my ass about your "set," even more than the way you ate your hamburgers by setting aside their perfectly good buns and neatly wrapping the patties in lettuce leaves. (The actual reason, by the way, that I accused you of being OCD.) You pitied practically every creature on earth, from Guatemalan coffee farmers to endangered forest gorillas, except for the men you lured into your beds. Depending on whether we seized you from behind (as you invariably dared us to) or requested a brief, loving kiss before we serviced you (as you mocked us for desiring), we all were either psychopaths or closet cases, would-be murderers or latent fags, and nothing in between.

Or maybe "borderline" is in between. Perhaps you don't remember, but that's the diagnosis you laid on me that night—a full hour before I said you were OCD. Did I deserve it? Not at that point, no. All I'd done was point out in the movie theater that for the price of the popcorns and diet sodas that you so patronizingly bought for both of us, even though I had my wallet out, I could have paid the teenage couple in front of us to put on a live-sex show back at your place and give us nude cocoa-butter massages afterward. "You'd like that kind of thing?" you asked me, and I said, "Who knows? But I moved here to find out."

Borderline. I didn't get it but I didn't mind, since there are certain disabling ideas that I'd rather die not understanding than to have to spend my life being undercut by. The word reminded me of two other terms that you used that night but which I haven't heard spoken since leaving New York: *pyrrhic* and *Kafkaesque*. Keep them, Amy. We don't need them here. Or whatever the heck they stand for. We're doing fine.

And you are also doing fine, I gather. (I searched your name at work the other day and learned that you're still writing your little stories about loyal animals and lousy humans.) That pleases me, Amy. As I said, I've changed. I eat much less meat now. I sold my antique sword. I've learned to appreciate modern German cinema, I've given up collecting, and I've befriended a former Marine Corps colonel who helped cook up several of the new "religions" that the Pentagon developed to influence Hollywood but has withdrawn its support for recently due to changing budget priorities. As for my novel, *Portal People*—which you so kindly helped me edit even after I borrowed your purse that night—it was lost by the Library of Congress, to whom I stupidly sent my only copies. Don't worry, though: The place is on my hit list. Someday fairly soon (July, perhaps, when my paintball squad plays in a tournament in Maryland) I plan to sneak into the library's main reading room with a kitchen match taped behind one ear and a balloon full of kerosene or diesel fuel tucked into my jeans. What a barbecue that will be! And what a menu! Baked Hemingway. Fried Fitzgerald. Roasted Thoreau. (I know you're "literary," Amy, but since all the great books will be safe on Google soon—including yours, let's hope—there's really no need for that flammable old castle.)

Seriously, though, I'm doing well. And maybe better than well, if things work out. I'm basically under contract at the moment to star in a major national ad campaign promoting the AidSat Active Angel service (which I urge you to subscribe to, since I assume that you still live alone and do a lot of walking after dark). But before we start filming, there is one tiny hurdle that I'm wondering if you can help me with: a background check.

I have no right to ask this, considering the grief I caused you, but if you have even a microdot of mercy for the guy who "hitchhiked" on your credit history and snapped a few photos of you on his phone that he sold to an amateur porn site in the Netherlands, you'll do me this favor: Forget you ever knew me. Either that, or remember (if you're ever asked to) that you knew another, better me. The Kent I'm becoming, not the Kent I was. And maybe you can ask Kathy to do likewise.

In closing, I must ask you to stop writing me and to stop expecting that I'll write you. This is for your protection as well as mine. Revisiting the past, I've found, is like dabbling in black magic—it seems a harmless rush at first, but you never know what dark spirits it will unleash. There are more souls than bodies on this planet, more ghosts than there are houses for them to haunt, and I'm content with the one inside me now. I'd rather not open a back door to those that I've shut out.

Eventually you'll see the ads I'll make, you'll hear about the stir I'll cause, and you'll understand that I'm not who you remember.

And thank God for that, I bet you're thinking!

Kent

P.S. **Borderline between what and what?** Don't answer.

29.

[Via courier]

Agent's Memo: Selkirk and I in a two-man paintball match, our arms and torsos encased in grass-stained pads, our feet clad in shoes whose cleats rip up the turf, our heads caged in Kevlar helmets equipped with face masks that leave only narrow slots for our fierce eyes and lend our combat an ancient, Roman feeling. I respect him, for once. The kid has footwork; he's never standing exactly where he seems to be. In the first twenty minutes I wasted a whole clip on him, shooting at afterimages, but gradually I learned to hold my fire. Now my opportunity has come. Our rifles have the heft of the real things, the complicated machining, the balanced barrels, and when we finally level them at each other after a lengthy tactical ballet of ducking and rolling and darting behind stacked hay bales, there's a moment of actual tenderness and terror, because I have the drop on him this time, and he knows it. He's wounded me twice in a row, but now it's my turn, and both of us know that it will be a kill shot.

Bright indigo to the chest. He's down. It's over.

Afterward, resurrected, in his street clothes, feeding a music CD into the slot of his pickup's dashboard stereo, he says to me, "Thanks for coming out today. I need this now and then. I need to die."

"You've found the right way to do it. Temporary."

" 'Hold on loosely,' like .38 Special says."

"Is that who this is?"

"It's Bo Bice. I voted for him."

I tell him I'm thirsty and name a bar whose middle booth I've rigged with mikes that will capture our words and the breaths between them, too. I wonder sometimes if Selkirk speaks in Morse code, through rhythmic silences and hesitations. I'll miss him, I realize. His nebulous charisma. Still, it's time to feed him to the fire. If this is a war, we need a body count.

There's a proposal I plan to make to Selkirk, and I sense he's in the mood to hear it. The world has been breaking his knuckles one by one, beginning last week with a call he got at home while placating angry exes by e-mail. He'd been at the task since Monday night, making amends, revising cover stories, and taking time out every ten or fifteen minutes to erase another false biography from another dim corner of the Web. Each time he pressed "delete" he shrank a little, and by Thursday evening, when the call came, there was barely enough of him left to grab the phone.

"Kent? It's Roger G. in human resources. About your background check."

"Is it complete?"

"We have some questions for you."

"Yes. Of course."

"This nurse in Wisconsin that you helped last March. This Sarah Flick. She contacted you socially. The photographs she sent were inappropriate. **As were the pictures that you then sent to her.**"

"I don't understand."

"Let's move this thing along. There's another AidSat subscriber, Sabrina Grant, whom we believe you've also dealt with socially."

"She lives in **my complex**."

"At present?"

"No."

"That's right. At present she resides in a facility."

"Where are you coming up with all this stuff?"

"Have you ever, while speaking to Miss Grant in the course of your formal AidSat duties, impersonated a female operator based in North Platte, Nebraska? Yes or no."

"Those are my only choices? May I explain, please?"

"And did you also, while posing as this operator, subject subscriber Grant to passive coverage for a period of eleven days, afterward seeking to conceal your mischief by claiming that the operator had died?"

"Sabrina Grant is insane. She's unreliable. I could sue you for what you're charging."

"She's not our source."

"Am I being fired? Is that where this is leading? Because if it is, I'm hiring a lawyer. I've suffered emotional traumas on this job. I've counseled subscribers who've died. Who've killed themselves. I've been on the line during acts of violence. It's all in my file. I'll claim a disability."

"That's not what we want."

"You're effing right you don't."

"We'd rather settle this matter between ourselves. Confidentially. Without a scandal."

"What would the scandal be?"

"That we ever hired you. We'd like you to take a week of paid vacation, Kent. We're pondering how to go forward with your case such that neither you nor AidSat suffers permanent damage or embarrassment. Chances are we'll suggest you get more therapy."

"What about my radio ad?"

"On hold."

"That hurts me."

"We're being generous, we feel. We're taking an enlightened corporate stance toward a valued member of our family who's faced a host of psychological challenges during his otherwise creditable tenure and whom we're hoping will make a full recovery."

"I appreciate it."

"As you should."

"Who tattled on me?"

"Relax. This day is done."

"You expect me to *sleep* tonight?"

"Just close your eyes."

Selkirk returned to his laptop when he hung up, purged his profile from another dating service, logged on to a costly Slovakia-based porn site specializing in older women on horseback, exited before the site had loaded, scanned the headlines on CNN.com, read a piece on the latest Canadian terror bust (by the way, congratulations, **Mounties**), ordered the movie *Nosferatu* from Netflix, and then spent seven minutes entering various combinations of search terms whose only common phrases were *blueprints* and *Library of Congress*. Finally, at 12:15 a.m., he placed the following cell phone call to Jesse, who'd left my bed just half an hour earlier without informing me of the vital news that she immediately shared with him:

"Let's get married tomorrow. I'm tired of this," he said.

"Of what, Cass?"

"Postponing destiny."

"Same here. That's why I'm trying to get pregnant."

"How?"

"I think you know how."

"But with who?"

"I'm sure you know that, too. I have to go."

"You love me, though."

"I'll love my child more."

Then back to the ladies-on-horseback site. Then bed. Then, in the morning a visit to the old colonel, who was recovering at home now in the company of Selkirk's dog, whose collar I'd implanted with a device at the VA hospital one night. Here's a sample of what the two men said, slightly edited for clarity, if clarity is possible between those characters:

"What was the ultimate goal, though?" Selkirk asked. They were talking Hollywood, as usual, with special reference to the Elvis Presley films that the colonel held up as an example of a "hegemonic myth-op."

"**The weaponization of culture**."

"Whose idea?"

"Ideas of this magnitude seldom have one author, but, should it ever be studied by historians, special credit will probably be assigned to Rear Adm. Bertrand Clayman Knox.

It came to him in a San Francisco safe house during a three-day lysergic-acid trip in July of 1956 while reading the recently published *On the Road*. Knox was what we called back then a nonspecific forward sensor. Basically, that's a professional hallucinator. He finally formalized the concept this way: 'Multiply the beatniks by the bomb, project from multistation global platform, and cultivate official distance from by designating un-American. Mao go bye-bye. Say good night, Nikita. Consult with Brits. Do not inform de Gaulle.' I've seen the original. Scribbled on a matchbook."

"I've never read *On the Road*. I've always meant to. He wrote it in like a week or two, they say."

"Once we supplied him with the proper medicines. Truth is, he'd been noodling around with it for years."

I mention all this to set a scene: Selkirk and I with a pitcher of dark beer and a basket of cream-cheese jalapeno poppers talking hypothetical grand arson. I, too, have a beef with the Library of Congress, I let on as we cooled down after the paintball duel. I said it relates to a family copyright that was insufficiently protected—a story that, incredibly, is true.

" 'It's the Real Thing' was your mother's?" Selkirk said.

"It referred to the cookies and caramel rolls she sold through a network of regional Indiana bakeries."

"That's a trademark, not a copyright. Your issue should be with the trademark office, Rob."

"Torch the whole city from end to end, I say, and let Vishnu sort it out. Or Allah. Or the Great Spirit. Pick your favorite."

"I don't have one," he said.

"You strike me as a mystic."

"Sort of. Sometimes."

"So, who's your favorite deity?"

"Not one that you'd be familiar with," he said.

I signaled the barmaid for another pitcher and a half order of atomic chicken wings. Alcohol and spices make Selkirk blush, I'd found, and a head full of blood is a head that I can work with.

"Can I be utterly candid with you, Kent?"

"That's up to you," he said.

"You're being monitored. You've been placed on a watch list along with several friends of yours. This isn't a joke, though. I know it for a fact."

This didn't appear to faze him as it should have. All he said to me was, "I had a hunch."

Then again, people his age have new assumptions. They've grown up believing in the orbiting eye, the subdermal microchip, the circling drone, and they're no more afraid of them than they are of moonlight. Perhaps that's because they're born onstage, these creatures, and the first thing they see is the snout of Daddy's Handycam. Their first steps, their first words, their first Little League at-bats are all directed toward the lens. In time, they have nothing inside them that hasn't been outside. No depths. No interiors. They have no use for them, even when they find themselves in crisis. Convinced that nothing can escape the probe, they've evolved to move sideways when threatened, instead of inward. Out of the old shot, toward the new shot. Crablike.

"I know this," I said, "because I'm the one who's watching you. Not that I want to or believe it's right to, but because it's my job. And, frankly, I despise it. It's barely legal, it serves no higher purpose, and the data it generates is largely meaningless and generally ignored. Except, of course, in retrospect, after there's been a disaster we didn't stop, but Congress insists that we could have, theoretically."

"You're not in telecom," said Selkirk. "You don't really work for Vectonal."

"No, I don't."

"You're still in the ATF or something."

"Something."

"I understand the firearms part," he said, "and maybe I kind of get it about the alcohol, but what's the great big panic about tobacco?"

I gave him the history lesson. It took five minutes. He made no move for the exits. No moves at all. Indeed, he looked calmer than I'd ever seen him. The chaos was finally being configured for him. The lunar craters were forming a face at last. No more akas. He had a name now. Kent Selkirk: Person of Interest.

I let him linger in his bliss, topped off our beers, then offered my proposal.

"I'm forty-five years old," I said. "High blood pressure, high cholesterol, high everything. I'd like a family. I'd like a house near water. They're offering early retirement in my department, and it's an attractive package. I want out, Kent. So this is my deal for you, with no fine print: Assure me you're harmless, that you're a nobody, and I'll write off our whole effort as a mistake, erase the recordings, shred the documents, and head off to make a baby with your ex as if this never happened and shouldn't have. All you have to do is say the word." That's when I reached for my hole card: the hidden microphone, which I placed on a napkin between us, beside the pitcher.

"A show of good faith," I said. "Handle it. **Examine it**. Take it away with you as a souvenir."

He fingered the thing. He stroked its silver belly.

"An AidSat ear jack is half this size," he said.

"Free markets trump the bureaucracy again."

"How long have you been studying me?"

"Three months."

"And all of it will go away?" I said.

"Filed under Z for zero. We'll leave you alone forever. All alone."

His eyes emptied out. It seemed this prospect scared him.

"This place is closing. The barmaid wants her tip. Say it clearly. 'I pose no danger, Rob.' Lift your chin, please. Speak into the mike."

It began then. **His full confession**.

30.

[Via courier]

Agent's Memo: Before I send along his grandiose ramblings, Selkirk asks that I print the following coordinates and pass them along to you, my bosses, for reasons that he insists you'll understand soon. I'm humoring him because, frankly, he exhausts me.

30N150W

31.

[Via courier]

Agent's Preface: *The following is a record of an interview with Person of Interest "Kent Ormand Selkirk." In return for agreeing to speak freely and without the presence of legal counsel concerning his background, activities, and plans, Selkirk made four unorthodox requests, all of which I chose to honor.*

1. *That our conversations be held in a superpremium king suite of the local W Hotel.*
2. *That he be provided with a computer and a high-speed Internet connection.*
3. *That he be able, at any time, to summon as a witness to our talks Lt. Col. Geoffrey Lark (Ret.).*
4. *That his statements to me be collected and preserved under a title of his choosing (which appears a few lines down).*

It should also be noted that the subject, despite showing frequent signs of agitation and psychological confusion, had access to neither alcohol nor drugs during the course of his "confession." Nor did he speak under duress. If at times his statements seem incoherent, this reflects not only his general mental state but also his peculiar ideas and attitudes concerning the nature of human language—specifically, his adherence to a pseudoscience known as **General Semantics** *and his belief in the power of so-called* **sigils**, *which he defined to me when we first sat down as "symbols that have wills. Words or images that don't just stand for something, but are capable of doing something." Then he offered to make a sigil for me. He printed his name on a sheet of hotel stationery and said, while drawing a star around the K, "Always remember:* **The map is not the territory**.*" He folded the piece of paper exactly six times, touched it to his forehead, shut his eyes, fell silent for a moment, and then reached across the space between our chairs and tucked the paper into my vest pocket, where he urged me to keep it throughout our interactions.*

I asked him if he was ready yet. He nodded. Then, on the blank screen of the computer positioned between us on a credenza, he typed in the title mentioned above:

A HISTORY OF PARTICKULAR EVENTS
PRESAGING THE **TIME-UNBINDING** OF THE NEW
AEON AS DICTATED BY AN ADEPT OF **THELEMA** AT
THE BEHEST OF ANUBIS, HIS **GUARDIAN ANGEL**

1.

If I told you where I was born, and when, and how much I weighed and what my parents named me, and even who my parents were, that would be hearsay. I can't vouch for hearsay. I'd rather confine myself to what I know, leaving out what I've been told or have inferred. If that frustrates you, I apologize, but I promised you the truth, Rob, nothing else, and there's not as much truth in this world as you may think. Indeed, there's hardly any—about which we may reliably speak, that is—and perhaps the main reason that I lured you here (and you were lured here, make no mistake) was to instruct you on this point. To begin with, you told me last night that you'd been "watching" me, but that isn't really the case, as it turns out. You were monitoring my communications, but my communications are no more "me" than the squeak of my tennis shoes on a hardwood floor is.

Be patient, Rob. You have a lot to learn, just as I did when I dwelled at your level.

A man, any man, is not the calls he makes, the letters he writes, or the e-mails he sends out. A man is what he knows. And the first thing that I knew in this life—knew independently, on my own, without taking someone else's word for it, as I did when I memorized the fifty states—was the pleasure I found in caressing an old black dachshund that the three people who called themselves my family referred to as Polly. I didn't call her anything. No need to. If I wanted her on my lap or on my bed, she came without being beckoned, by and large; and when she didn't come, I didn't command her to, which only seemed fair, since she never gave me commands. Everyone else I knew gave me orders constantly, which may be the reason that I had no desire to tickle them under their chins or scratch their butts. The arthritic black dachshund was unique, and so were my feelings for her. This I knew. And it's all that I knew, truly *knew*, for several years.

But then the two people whose presence in our house seemed to define what I'd learned to call "my family" decided that they were not *each other's* family and set to work dividing up their property, including me and the slender, red-haired girl whom, to satisfy custom, I called my sister. We weren't split physically, but temporally, in terms of weekends and vacation days. The effect would have been the same if we'd been guillotined and our body parts sealed in separate Ziploc bags. The black dachshund, however, could not be thus apportioned, and since neither my mother-woman nor my father-man wished to care for the animal alone, it went someplace. I never found out where. I heard stories—about a "shelter," about a "ranch," about an elderly lady across town—but I didn't know which one to believe or how to go about investigating them.

That's a problem. The largest problem, really. Though we're told by the fashionable thinkers that life provides no answers, only questions, the actual situation is just the opposite. The world is awash in answers, it overflows with them, while the questions that generate them are rather few. (To prove this, just enter the following short sentence into any sophisticated search engine—*What are the causes of borderline personality disorder?*—and press the return key. Answers without end.) In the case of the vanishing black dachshund, all of the answers I got seemed plausible and one of them seemed, quite possibly, correct (my sister's, "They left it in the Target parking lot"), but none of them addressed the central problem.

If the dog was gone, was the feeling gone as well?

Because I wanted it back, I decided to call the feeling "love" instead of "what it was like to rub my dachshund." Then I gave my invention certain properties, chief among them mobility. Love moves. It moves from things that are gone to things that aren't gone, and all I had to do in life, all anyone has to do in life, was to find those things. Or, as the greeting cards insist is preferable, to let those things find me.

I tried.

I tried for years, Rob. Harder than anybody ever has.

I tried first with a hamster that my mother gave me because it cost less to feed than other pets, but it lacked a chin for me to tickle.

I tried with a bicycle, but it was stolen.

I tried with a character on a TV show, but he didn't respond to me when I spoke to him or spell my name right when I finally met him at a store where he was signing his books, which I later found out that he hadn't even written.

I tried with a girl named Lara in junior high, but Lara loved Bo, and one night she told me so.

I tried with Bo. He slugged me in the ribs.

I tried with two Susans, three Elizabeths, a Moira, a Tammi, and Tammi's little sister—all during a single freshman year.

I tried with the all-male school that I was sent to when the school with the girls in it expelled me for following one of them into her house one night and yelling at her for telling another one that I preferred a third one, which wasn't true.

I tried with the planet, our lovely planet Earth, and with all the rare, threatened creatures that inhabit it, especially a certain species of salmon. But one summer night in British Columbia, while vandalizing a dam with several friends who were also trying to love the Earth, I watched as a boy who looked a lot like me was swept underwater by giant dam machinery and torn into pieces so small they never surfaced and couldn't be found by a team of divers, either.

I tried with the dead boy's college ID card, which he'd left with his shoes on the front seat of my car.

It went on for years, from Tampa to Milwaukee, from Amy to Kathy, from muscle car to mountain bike, and then, when I could afford an Apple computer, from Friendster to MySpace. It tired me out. When the people I tried to love failed to love me back, I altered myself to make myself more lovable, and when they found out that they loved an altered me, they went away in search of someone else. Sometimes the someone else they came across was yet another altered me, which they'd realize when we met in person, causing a lot of trouble I won't go into. And sometimes the people I found when I searched further were the same people I'd tried to love before, with different hair, new nicknames, and changed hobbies.

Finally, I gave up. And only then, Rob, thanks to **a man whom we both know**, but whom only I know well, I was shown my original error and set free, just as we hope to set you free before much longer, which is why we've worked so hard to bring you here.

There's a lot more to tell, but I need my guru now. He's waiting for you with his dog at his apartment. Go get him. I'll be here.

32.

[MyStory.com]

You've left me alone in the hotel room, Rob, and driven off toward Colonel Geoff's apartment, deeper into the city of false artifacts. Undercover men—what slaves you are! You're slaves to your superiors, who abuse and oppress you because they're slaves themselves. You're slaves to your disguises, which force you to wear the suit of mediocrity. Mostly, though, you're slaves to your suspicions, which belong not to you but to we who raise suspicion.

And who, these days, can raise it with a few keystrokes, as the colonel set out to do last January when he borrowed Sabrina's phone (poor dupe) while she was boiling lentils in his kitchen. This is the text message that started everything, the provacative sentence that made the colonel lord and fed the stream of other suggestive utterances—many of them mine—that have kept him lord:

> Back in position, operating freely, living like a bloody sheikh, and having a goddamn blast— praise heaven!

He forwarded this to three recipients and three types of devices, whose numbers and addresses came from a long list that I'd picked, almost at random, off the Net. A cell phone used by the madam of a brothel located near a Nevada air force base, a BlackBerry belonging to a publicist, and the "Contact Us" section of the home page of the American Kennel Club in New York. The spell took forty or fifty seconds to cast and exactly nine weeks to bring the entity that it was meant to conjure forth. A magickal welcome, Rob. The colonel knew they'd send someone, and it was you. The only surprise was the route our invitation (and the phone number attached to it) followed to your boss's desk. We expected that it would be snatched from the ionosphere—and perhaps it was—but it was also, we're quite confident, passed along terrestrially by the same hot-blooded minuteman at the AKC who immediately texted back as follows to our decoy's pink Samsung: "i scan the blogs i visit drudge im hip to codes back channels cyber dead drops and say fu 2 all u sobs 4 all the usa."

But maybe you weren't privy to much background stuff. Maybe your box is at the flowchart's edge, with barely any inward-pointing arrows, and all they put in your valise was Sabrina's name and address. That was the colonel's first impression, at least, as we followed you through a Whole Foods after I'd flushed you from the brush by illegally asking Peter P. for AidSat's files on Sabrina Grant and then, apropos of absolutely nothing, by repeatedly bringing her name during Active Angel calls. And here on MyStory, of course, my hotline to the Potomac.

"Not the type they lavish long briefings on," said the colonel, watching you squeeze honeydews. "I think they gave us Agent 000. Licensed to kill, but has to check with Mommy. That Timex with the Velcro strap definitely doesn't fire darts. He hasn't approached you yet?"

"Not yet."

"But he's the one?"

"He joined my health club a few days ago. He lifts the same amount of weight no matter what muscle group he's working on. Leg press or triceps extension—fifty pounds." We rounded the corner of the soy milk aisle and there you were again, scooping loose protein powder into a Baggie. You wanted sinew. Sad. Next stop, fish oil for a quicker brain. Then over to skin care for a jar of eye cream and a file to smooth your heels and elbows.

"**Preparing for mummification,**" the colonel said.

When you left me behind at the hotel here, I assume that you placed me under guard, perhaps by the room-service waiter who brought our dinners but couldn't answer my questions about the mushrooms mixed with the wild-rice pilaf. Peace, my sentries. Through studying under Colonel Geoff—whom I've known somewhat longer than my writings have indicated—I've learned to assume that I'm always under guard and, more important, always under scrutiny. Every word that I speak, every message that I write, and every action that I perform (with certain sacred exceptions) is partly addressed, or in some way conscious, of a hovering third party—if not an infinite host of them.

"Lead the Trespasser," is the colonel's maxim.

The idea has an interesting history. It comes from a treatise that the colonel cowrote during his service days with a Princeton social anthropologist and an ex-Communist Jewish screenwriter. The colonel nicknamed the myth-op behind the document "Destroy All Saucers!" Its goal was to change **the standard Hollywood Martian**—that stiff-legged, monosyllabic big-eyed bug that some in the military were convinced was a subversive caricature of **the dronelike Cold War soldier**—into a more enchanting, more personable **"Interstellar Emissary."** Unlike the Martians, who traveled to our planet full of absolutist zeal, intent on either dominating us or saving us from our own ignorance, the IE merely wanted to know humanity, mix with it, and obscurely reassure it that all is well Out There. The Pentagon funded the project, the colonel told me, because its deepest thinkers had grown convinced that moviegoers unconsciously identified beings from space with our nation's governing class.

That's where "Lead the Trespasser" came in. In the script that the myth-op hoped to generate (the many scripts, that is, since the IE was a template for all new spacemen, not a one-time-only alien), the earthlings would shrink from the IE at first, and some of them, inevitably, would attack it. These fools would be instantly incinerated, unleashing even greater world anxiety. Soon, however, a wise man would appear and help human beings adopt a subtler strategy toward the visitor. They'd let the IE circulate among them while carrying on with their daily lives. They'd test it, too. They'd drum up a scare about a worldwide drought and hope the IE would show pity and send the rains.

Finally, toward the end, the earthlings would acknowledge the IE and admit to it what they'd been up to. Angry over being toyed with, it would prepare to annihilate mankind. Then the wise man would step in again. He'd suggest that instead of reacting with primal fury, the IE ought to show some civilized respect for an intelligent society capable of engaging it in play. Perhaps a new relationship was possible?

The IE could remain as a sort of grand custodian and media-tor of disputes, and mankind would supply it with X (X being some substance that the IE required to survive but had run out of back where it was born).

That was the myth-op. The colonel said it failed. Yes, the portrayal of movie spacemen softened ("A bit too much in **that Kubrick thing**," he said, "though I did love the fruity purring of that computer"), but the genre soon regressed into juvenile spectacle. Worse, not a single apothegm or dictum from his intensively researched treatise was ever uttered on-screen. This embittered him. Especially after that ponderous silliness "Use the Force, Luke" gained such renown.

I've discussed this matter at such length because it explains, I hope, my fearlessness as I sit here at my keyboard, disclosing to you, the imminent third party, all that we, the Anubists, know and will. Soon, our whole project will be plain. It's not a plot; it's a procedure. It's not a conspiracy; it's a practice. That all can master, in their own degrees, but only a few of us have pledged our lives to.

And then there's you, Rob. The naked undercover man. The incorporated intruder. Who crashed a party posing as a caterer but still doesn't see that it's his name on the cake.

On both cakes, actually.

The "Welcome Home" cake and the "Bon Voyage" cake.

Which cake we'll serve will be up to you, our guest.

Right now you're driving north. Because I'm not at work and can't connect to the pill-size AidSat ear jack chewing-gummed inside your dashboard vent, I don't know what you're playing on his stereo. If experience is any guide, it's either the Eagles' *Greatest Hits* or Sinatra's *In the Wee Small*

Hours. I'm grateful to you for exposing me to the Sinatra, and I'm grateful as well for *Aguirre, the Wrath of God,* which I can't say I've managed to watch yet without fast-forwarding but whose title is like a mantra to me now. Its silent repetition clears my mind. Perhaps that's all minds are made of: words and tunes. I try to let them guide me. Don't be surprised if six months or so from now a talkative young man named Frank Aguirre starts acting up in Yahoo! chat rooms, listing his favorite slasher films on Netflix, barraging his senators with moody e-mails, and slowly cross-referencing himself to life the way Kent Selkirk did.

I hope it's the Sinatra that you have on as you turn left onto the colonel's street. More truth in it. More loss. More need.

Sing with him. Ache with him, Rob.

It might just save you.

33.

[G-mail.com]

KentSelkirk@gmail.com

Dear Kent,

It's been twelve hours since I left you, but perhaps because you believe you're "under guard," you're still in the hotel, I notice, living high off the in-room dining menu and enjoying *The Da Vinci*

Code on pay-per-view. You've also been online, I see, since we parted. I expected that. And so, rather than driving to the colonel's and further humoring your dreary fantasies of DC Comics omnipotence, I rode the elevator five floors down to a second room I'd rented, showered, mixed a cocktail from the minibar, spent forty minutes on the phone cooing and bickering with Jesse, and then logged on to MyStory.com to read the post that I knew you'd start composing the moment I left you to yourself.

Before I address the contents of your post and tell you whom I've seen and what I've done today, allow me to extend my sympathy, Kent. You're a young man who can't bear to be alone, and yet, because of **the way you find companionship**, you almost always are. Your failure to even partially commit to the world of flesh has turned you into a line of walking code programmed to seek attention electromagnetically. Having shed your human capacity for human attachment, you'll never go bats the way Sabrina did recently, or the way Colonel Geoff did many years ago, but you'll soon face an even grimmer fate: unencumbered freedom. And you will have achieved this freedom by a new means. Revolutionary incoherence. The inability to be grasped by anyone, let alone by me, a middle-aged agent of the state who has his own problems warming to other people.

Still, I predict that you'll mourn me when I'm

gone. Big Brother was your last chance to have a family, Kent, but he has despaired of learning even your name, or even the screen name that you use most frequently. He has reached one conclusion, though, which will allow him to depart contented: You are not a threat to law and order.

You just choose, for some reason, to live like one.

As I said, I reviewed your latest post. I laughed at every line. Particularly amusing was your claim that, in league with the colonel, your lord and wizard, you drew me here for some chilling ritual purpose shrouded in the lore of ancient Egypt. (I looked up Anubis: a quasi-canine deity associated with graves and corpses, whose dog-headed hiero-glyph could be your portrait, Kent.) What a dun-geon of ominous nonsense your mind's become! Is there something I'm not aware of about computer land that drives its denizens to bogus sorcery? **Why does the consummate product of rationality foster this dragon-haunted spiritualism?**

In any case, I slept dreamlessly and soundly after closing your post. No nocturnal visitations. I woke, dressed, downed a quattro cappuccino, han-dled some difficult official business, and drove to the Center for New Integrity, where I'd arranged for a visit with Sabrina. In your post you portrayed her as the patsy through whom you attracted me, the FB Eye, but I see the poor damsel for what she is: a soul that has starved itself in every way, desper-ate to be fed. You threw her some crumbs, but they were indigestible, made of silicon and polymers. They passed right through her, and she was empty again.

I met her in the patients' dining room, where she was locked in psychological combat with a plate of eggs and minicroissants. "Like this," I said, raising a pastry to my lips. She shuddered. She couldn't do it. A plainclothes counselor stood by, pecking surreptitious notes into a device in her left palm.

"Kent says to say hello to you," I lied. "The colonel, too."

"They're fiends," she said.

"They wish."

She shook her head. She shook it more, I mean. It was shaking plenty already. Her whole body was. "Sometimes, when I'm sketching in art therapy, they manifest themselves to me," she said.

"As malevolent dog-men?"

"Exactly."

"That's dementia. That's what you're here to be cured of. And you will be. If you stick with your artwork and nibble a croissant."

"What are you doing here?" she asked me. I hadn't noticed it before, but her spine has an S-curve, like a straightened paper clip. It unkinks when she's on alert and she grows taller.

"I don't want to threaten your recovery by going into detail, dear, but suffice it to say that I represent a group that identified you as a danger sometime back. This morning, after spending several months trying to discover what sort of danger, I tendered my resignation to my supervisors and informed them of my plan to marry Jesse, relocate to a seaside golf resort, and pen a fictional memoir of my service."

"Will anyone I know be in it?"

"Not specifically. As I say, I intend to make it up. I might have a character called Sabrina, though, because it's a name I find uniquely resonant."

"Will it be titled *The Cornering*?"

"Don't think so."

"*The Osiris Parallel?*"

"That was my thought: something Ludlum-ish. I want the thing to sell." I held the pastry to her mouth, and she nicked it with her incisors, which was progress. The lurking counselor noted her feat and left.

"I haven't told you why I'm sorry yet. After faxing him my letter of resignation, my superior called me, in person—which he never does—and, by way of coaxing me to stay, he made a strange admission about your case. Strange because it exposed his fallibility."

"I'm not a terrorist after all," she said.

"No, but there's a negligible chance that 'Sabrina M. Gray' may be. Unless, as seems much likelier, she's merely an Illinois soybean farmer's wife. She bought a great deal of fertilizer last winter—

potentially explosive ammonium nitrate—and because it's a substance the law keeps track of these days, she had to sign for the purchase, and she was sloppy, and. . . ."

Sabrina nodded. She'd finally stopped quivering. There's nothing more reassuring to the unstable than learning that they've been extensively investigated.

"Oh, well," Sabrina said.

"Oh, well. That's the attitude."

"In bed one night not long before I stabbed him, Kent told me that you were a 'portal emissary' sent here either by 'Horus or Thoth himself' to prevent him from issuing orders over AidSat to 'Unbind the one scroll.' But I guess not," she said.

"It'll be tough to break it to him," I said.

"When will you?"

"Very soon."

And now I have.

Awaiting your disconsolate reply (while packing a suitcase before I jet to Maui and wed your ex-girlfriend by torchlight at the Four Seasons while wearing nothing but bathing trunks and flip-flops),

Your retired shadow,
"Rob Robinson"

34.

[G-mail.com]

Robrob@gmail.com

Dear Dead Man,

It's not the way that you people break and enter that has always bothered me, it's the way that you leave things broken when you exit.

I think **intruders** should have to stay.

I think that should be their **punishment**.

But now you've flown off. Toward Hawaii via yesterday. Back here on the mainland dawn approaches, but out where your plane is, several time zones west of me (as shown on the AidSat GPS receiver that's linked to the ear jack I stashed in Jesse's carry-on), it's still last night, and moonless, and all black. Look down through that scratched plastic window beside your seat, Rob. Now look up. No difference, really, is there? The quotesmiths tell us that the eyes deceive us, but since everything else deceives us, too, that's not the eye's peculiar weakness. Its weakness is this: It's dependent on a light source.

But you're in the dark now. You're out of range. Which is why you're unable to read this message—

the only one that I've ever sent to anyone that was worth intercepting, finally. Conventional signals can't reach you where you sit, though; only powerful satellite transmissions such as the one that's about to shock and shake you. It's coming, Rob. It's coming from the sky, brought to you by the same big AidSat satellites that handle a hundred cries for help per minute. That unlock the car doors. That stop the vomiting. That put the children to sleep.

Your seat may also be used as a flotation device.

That's the only advice that I can give you.

Now let's move ahead with your Unbinding.

Since we've already removed your eyes, let's eliminate your sense of touch. Touch requires an object to excite it, Rob, and in your case, that object has been your seatmate, Jesse, a woman whom you believe belonged to me once. This notion stimulates you more than she does. When you kiss her, stroke her, fondle her—but especially when you thrust way up inside her—you're pushing me out, you think. You're snaking the drain. Except that I was never in there, Rob. Hundreds of others have been, but never me. The colonel, who has been paying her by the week, tells me she serviced the Marine Corps brass once—sometimes a half dozen at a time. She loves to take orders, he says, and never asks questions, no matter how elaborate the mission.

I think her working name is Violet Dawn.

And I know there are plastic explosives in her carry-on.

This is a detail that you'll fully appreciate, after I've numbed your senses of taste and smell. I'll do this by answering, factually, the questions that you decided weren't worth pursuing once your attention shifted to the beach. Though in truth, your attention was always on the beach. You government fellows are like that, Rob. You're the original Puritan party boys, always looking ahead to the big shindig that will be justified once you've had your war. To celebrate in the grand American style, with beer and bikinis and bottle rockets, you need to feel that you worked first, that you sacrificed.

I'm about to assist you in that regard. First, though, I need to tell you who I am.

My name is Kent Selkirk, but soon enough it won't be, and just four years ago it was Cass B. Kirksell, the unsuccessful fairgrounds blender demonstrator. Cass succeeded another C-named youth: Curtis Ormand, a kid with a shaved head who delivered cocaine by moped in San Francisco. I liked being Curt because he cut a figure, zipping past the Transamerica Pyramid with tens of thousands of dollars' worth of stimulants stuffed in the lining of his red saddlebag. He went to work with the stockbrokers at dawn, and regarded himself as a lubricated ball joint in an enormous economic mechanism that also included the bankers who used his coke to help them through their global trading days. Breakfast in London, lunch in New York City, no real dinner, and drinks in Tokyo.

Surfing that time wave requires strong pick-me-ups. If a guy tuckers out and topples off his board, the sea picks it up and slams it against his skull. (You're about to know the feeling, Rob.)

I'll stop at Curtis, but I go back, believe me. I go back many years. And then I stop. I stop with a kid whose real name doesn't matter, since his schoolmates rarely used it. Because of a nervous habit he'd developed after his parents disposed of his pet dachshund in a Target parking lot, this kid with buckteeth (only one of which was white) took to biting and gnawing at his fingers, and for this he was called "Chewnucca."

Chewnucca Smith.

It's a name that I've used only once in the last decade—while scolding Twist for peeing on my futon ("Bad, Chewnucca! *Bad!*")—but it's who I am and who I'll always be. I gave Twist to Colonel Geoff that night because I had no right to punish a dog for it.

Because I'm a dog, too. We all are, I've discovered. We come when our masters shout our names. When I was a young teen, my masters were my classmates. When I became an old teen, at military school, my masters were men of stiff bearing. Yours still are. I, though, answer only to myself now.

"Gnobedience." It's one of Colonel Geoff's terms. He coined it with another psy-ops officer,

Lt. Col. Michael Aquino, who is arguably America's leading **satanist** and runs the **Temple of Set** in San Francisco. (All true, I swear—just click and see.) I met Colonel Geoff in my year beside the Bay, longer ago than I've ever quite let on, before he quit the cult and moved back here to start his own, much more exclusive sect. But you don't believe in rebels of his dimensions. You're as scared as the next secret agent about the plots, but you still have trouble spotting the plotters. Allow me to profile them for you. They don't want justice. They don't want vengeance. They don't want blood. They want what all good Americans are supposed to want but tend to give up fighting for at some point.

Liberty, I guess.

I'm sorry, Rob, but whatever your bosses told you about the clerical error behind your mission here (the supposed confusion about Sabrina's last name, which I suspect was invented by the big boys to hide the fact that they were tricked), the truth is that you were summoned by the colonel. He knew just which words to send over just which wires (*bloody*, *sheikh*, and *heaven* typed into Sabrina's Samsung flip phone) to call you to us like a dog.

Perhaps I'll buzz you now for one last sat-chat. At the hotel the other night, I slipped another ear jack in your briefcase. There. It's turned on. It's vibrating. Pick up, Rob.

"What the hell?" you say. "Who is this? Kent?"

"I think we've known each other long enough that you can call me 'What's-his-face.' "

"You incredible nutcase. You never shut up, do you?"

"Where are you?"

"Locked in the bathroom of a Boeing. Passengers aren't supposed to use their phones here."

"This isn't a phone. It's the longest fuse on Earth. . . ."

"I'm flushing this AidSat thing down the goddamn toilet unless you tell me exactly why you're calling."

"Because you listen."

"My mistake."

"No, your mistake," I say, "is disobeying."

"Disobeying what?"

"Your master's voice."

I pressed a red key and I took another call then, because it's my job and because they never end.

ALSO BY WALTER KIRN

THUMBSUCKER

Meet Justin Cobb, "The King Kong of oral obsessives" (as his dentist dubs him) and the most appealingly bright and screwed-up fictional adolescent since Holden Caulfield. Always funny, sometimes hilariously so, *Thumbsucker* is an utterly fresh and all-American take on the painful process of growing up.

Fiction/978-0-385-49709-1

MISSION TO AMERICA

Mason LaVerle was raised in a tiny, isolated Montana sect, the church of the Aboriginal Fulfilled Apostles. But the Apostles face a dwindling membership, so Mason is sent on an outreach operation to bring back converts. As he discovers shopping malls, fast food, and faster women, the forces of faith and of America collide, leading Mason to the brink of missionary madness.

Fiction/978-1-4000-3101-6

UP IN THE AIR

Ryan Bingham's job as a Career Transition Counselor—he fires people—has kept him airborne for years. Although he despises his line of work, he has come to love the culture of what he calls "Airworld," finding contentment within pressurized cabins and anonymous hotel rooms. With perception, wit, and wisdom, *Up in the Air* establishes Kirn's place as one of our most important young novelists.

Fiction/Literature/978-0-385-72237-7

ANCHOR BOOKS
Available at your local bookstore, or call toll-free to order:
1-800-793-2665 (credit cards only).